LAST SEEN AT...

BY
SUSAN N. WILLIAMS

People have a lot to say about lives they've never lived. —Anonymous

CHAPTER 1

Mid-States Psychiatric Hospital

I am alone in this cold, stark room. The irony of that isn't lost on me. That's how I've felt my entire life, even more so in my married life. When Dr. Phillips comes to my room, he and his team explain that the stress I endured over the last year is too much for my brain to handle. My body and brain need rest. I wish my brain would listen to Dr. Phillips' advice and the pill he says will help. My mind keeps racing, and I can't make it stop.

I am here to think and to heal. I came here on my own because I know this is the right thing to do. My entire life, I did only the right things. But doing so has left me empty, unfulfilled and without passion. I guess that's the thanks I get for being the good wife, daughter, employee, or whatever else someone needed me to be.

As soon as we first wrote to one another, I knew he was the one I had always needed. I had found this one person in the world who understood me. My entire being wanted him and the intimacy we created. I never imagined a love so deep. We talked for hours and I always wanted more. We debated our thoughts and opinions, shared our dreams, and bared our souls. I didn't know I was starving for love until I met him. I never felt so close to anyone, ever.

No one should pity me. I don't pity myself. I was blessed with other things. I worked hard, focused on pharmacy school, established my career with a great company, married, and later, raised children. Other people were doing the same; I wasn't unique. I certainly wasn't special. I was too busy caring for everyone and everything to think about what I wanted. If someone needed something planned, cooked, cleaned, organized, funded, perfected, I was your girl. No one ever cared to ask me if I wanted to; if it needed done, I just did it. After years of work, I've earned what I have: the big house in a desirable neighborhood, a great job and a wonderful family. But I had no one in my life who had a clue or gave a damn about what I wanted. Now he is mine forever, and nothing has been the same since.

I lie here, staring at the stark walls without any artwork or curtains. They wouldn't want me to hurt myself, I guess. That's just it though. They don't have to worry about that. I would never do that; it might cause someone else more work or make them uncomfortable. I laugh a little to myself about that. I would probably write an apology note. "So sorry for my mental illness and the mess I have made. Please accept my apologies and this nice bouquet of flowers....".

My whole life, I did the right things, never wanting to upset anyone but now I feel so empty. No one ever tells you that might happen. They only say be a good citizen, a good example, a good whatever you want to put in that blank, and good things will happen. But I have found without a doubt that is a lie. My mind is racing. Did my life make me a lonely, desperate woman? Someone who should be taken advantage of or deceived? Does my naivete and belief that true love exists make me a fool? I can't and won't accept that. I still believe in love and the good humanity that exists within us all. I believe in us. He became my best friend and my soul mate. Now he will remain only mine forever. I should be happy, right?

As I lie here, I hold my stomach, waiting for this morning's bout of nausea to subside. Thinking how simple and quiet my life used to be, that is, until I met him. I was born and raised in the middle of America and attended a state university. I never lived more than a day's drive from my childhood home in Nebraska. I always dreamed of travel and meeting people like him, but never did. There was always something important that needed to be done and someone needed me to do it. In my hometown, people are busy working and trying to make ends meet. There isn't much time for travel or discussions about any topic other than the weather. But with him, it's different. I come alive when we talk. That's a phrase that he uses, and I think that's exactly the right way to describe it. Any topic is fair game for us, but we both especially like economics and business. He is fascinated by the monetary system in the US and Europe. He asks intelligent questions about investing and finance. He seems sincerely concerned if I am saving enough, investing, and avoiding taxes. He offers advice about how I should hold my assets to have financial freedom.

I find myself so intrigued by his experiences and his opinions. We suggest our favorite books and authors to one another. Unlike my husband, he is genuinely interested in my perspective of the topics. Even when we don't agree, our discussions and debates make me appreciate and admire his intelligence.

I belong to a book club in my small community. I love the discussion and new perspectives that are revealed every meeting. I love to learn and see others' point of view. My children sometimes say I'm a nerd but smile at me when they roll their eyes. The fact that he is well read and loves to discuss new ideas is another one of my favorite things about him. I love to hear about places he has traveled and what he has seen all over the world. We have so many things in common though. I still can't believe I was lucky enough to fall in love with someone like him.

So, over the past year, why was I, a married mother of 3, chatting with him? I'll tell you. It's because he completely awakened me; he made me feel alive again. He aroused my intellect and every part of my body. He made me desire again. We could talk for hours and never run out of things to say. As I told him many times, he is brilliant, a fascinating mystery, and he completely intrigues me…. but now I am here alone.

Grace

My family celebrates at home during the holidays. Years ago, our extended families all agreed to avoid the holiday travel chaos. Rather than gathering on the traditional days, we all assemble on a December weekend that is convenient for everyone's work schedule. It's a bit more relaxed than most families, but it works for us. That's why I was just hanging out with my kids and had nothing to do on the day after Christmas. They were watching their favorite holiday movie, Elf, like they do every year. As usual, my husband was working in his office.

I was wrapped up in a blanket, in my favorite chair, only partially listening to the movie. My teenagers have watched the movie so many times, I think we can all recite most of it. As I was scrolling through Harvard Business articles on a professional networking group, I noticed a connection request pop up. This isn't infrequent as I try to stay active on professional social media. Often, it's job opportunities from recruiters, a webinar I might be interested in, or another individual with a similar career or interests.

This was different. A US Air Force officer, Andrew E. Bronnan. I was intrigued. Why would he want to connect with me, a pharmaceutical manager? I scrolled through his profile. He looked harmless enough. Judging from his profile, he was a strikingly handsome man with quite a successful career. He had clearly studied and worked hard to be in that position. His peppery gray hair was neatly trimmed, and I instantly liked the tiny dimple in his chin. He appears confident and in charge. His hometown is somewhere in Florida. Ok, I accept, click, done. Where's the harm in that? I went back to reading until time for bed.

I read until I was sleepy. My husband always watches TV or does paperwork before he falls asleep. Rather than coming to bed, he often sleeps in his office or in the living room. I am used to this and don't take it personal. I despise a television in my bedroom. I absolutely cannot sleep with it on, so this arrangement works well for both of us. It also means I am alone, which I don't mind. But it makes me wonder if this is what our marriage has become and will remain for the rest of our lives. When we do make love, my husband immediately goes back to paperwork or checking Facebook in his office as soon as it's over. Most of the time, I'm fine with his absence. It gives me an opportunity to read, work late or just sleep without fighting for the blankets or hearing him snore. But is this normal? I honestly don't know. I know of couples who have their own bedrooms. I have acquaintances who take vacations separate from their husbands. We couldn't afford that, and I wouldn't know how to even bring it up, but it sounds fine to me. How is it any different than my day-to-day life now?

I have three children: my wonderful, sweet babies. Two beautiful, smart girls, Sarah, and Tabitha (we call her Tabby) and then my youngest, my son, Seth. They try to do their best in high school, have summer jobs, and are just great kids. They are my world. Of course, they are typical teenagers, sometimes moody, and they argue with each other. But I am proud to say they are becoming wonderful young adults.

My career is demanding and often pulls me away or I bring work home with me. I have a graduate degree in pharmacy with a minor in finance. I manage a large team in a successful company. I also teach a graduate class at a private university. A homeowner with a bit of land, the so-called American dream. It is so predictable, but so… vanilla. I did the right things, invested, read to my children, gardened, prayed, yoga, all of it. My husband has a successful architect firm, and we have a good relationship and never fight. Our lovemaking isn't frequent like it used to be, but still nice. I'm comfortable.

I sleep with my phone on the nightstand, the exact thing that sleep experts say not to do. I never know when an employee may call in the early hours or I will get an important client's email from another time zone. I am awake early every morning, checking messages and starting my day before my feet hit the floor. I didn't get to this career level by sleeping through the night.

At 2am, I get a notification that someone has messaged me on LinkedIn. It's him, the air force guy. The standard new connection hello. Ok, "hello back to you, I hope you are doing well." I go back to sleep.

Then another message, "I enjoyed viewing your profile. I would like to know more about your work."

I rub the sleep from my eyes and reply, "Ok, what would you like to know?" After that initial question, I was shocked we chatted about our careers for almost an hour. He then said he needed to go but told me to take care. I wished him the same.

CHAPTER 2

A few days pass since that first message and the children are still on holiday break from school. I enjoy a few quiet days off, just being at home with them and my husband. The weather is mild, and we get to be outside a bit, playing with the dog, going for walks, and just enjoy our time together. This is perfect for me. I love peaceful moments like this. There is enough stress and drama at work, I want my private life to be quiet. The girls and I spend time baking and decorating cookies. My husband works shorter days over the holiday break. He and Seth have been battling on the Playstation 4 Seth received for Christmas. The girls and I jump when startled by their sudden outbursts throughout the game.

This time at home with my family makes me dread returning to work. A holiday break is just what I need to recharge right now. I love my job, but it takes a lot of energy to get FDA approval, bring new drugs to the market and train the sales team. I like that big picture planning, especially the strategic development of a product or service line. I had worked hard to get to this level in my career. I loved the fast pace, meeting deadlines, fighting for the resources my department needed to advance our product. That is what keeps my mind engaged.

What I don't tolerate is the occasional drama from my employees or feeling like I must babysit adults. I hire people based on their ability and intelligence. I will never understand why some employees can't weave professional conduct in their repertoire. I can always train someone to a task or workflow, but I can only do so much to teach you how to be nice and collegial. There are literally thousands of leadership and management books written on dysfunctions of teams and employee engagement. There's Ted talks, social media blogs; all about how to get people to work with others. Didn't we learn this in kindergarten?

I enjoy learning from other leaders about these struggles. Sometimes, it makes me feel better; that I have it pretty good compared to some and I should be thankful. After a particularly difficult issue with an employee, a Human Resources representative told me that if addressing these issues and mentoring the employee doesn't keep you up at night, then it's time to get out of management. Regardless, it doesn't make the day to day stress any easier. Andrew shares a similar mindset and approach to leadership as mine. He understands how stressful it is leading people and being responsible for the success of the team. I enjoy our discussions about those issues.

The day Andrew messaged me again, I had just terminated an employee for conduct. I had done all I could do; the employee refused to take ownership of his actions or be guided to correct behavior. It was a difficult termination, and I was exhausted. I was headed home, glad that the long day was behind me. Like every parent, it was time to start full time job number two. I still had to record a lecture for a class I teach, cook dinner, and help the children with homework. Finally arriving home, I sat in my car for a moment and check other messages and saved his for last.

"Hi, I keep thinking about our conversation. I would like to know you better. May I email you?" I stared at the message for a moment. What does this mean? Professionally? Surely, I must tell him I'm married, right? Or will he think I'm assuming something?

I answered, "I'd like to keep our chats here if you don't mind. But I did enjoy our conversation."

"I did too. I just had more to ask so I wanted to write it all out, that was all. If you want to keep our chat here, that's fine," he says.

Hmmm, he does seem sincere. But I don't think I should give him my personal email so I type, "I'll give you my work email and you can write to me there."

"Perfect, I'll write to you soon," he answered quickly.

CHAPTER 3

Later, after most of the day's work is complete, I'm lying in bed. It's almost midnight but I am still awake. My mind wanders to the air force guy. What is he going to ask? Am I doing something wrong by talking him? I glance at the other side of the king-sized bed. Empty again. I frown at the space and run my hand over the high-quality Egyptian cotton bedding. Then I turn away to face the wall. I usually am pretty good at blocking out the loneliness. Yet tonight it's very real. I don't think it's actually my husband that I miss. I miss the pillow talk at the end of a long day. I miss how it feels so perfect to lay in the arms of a man I love. No, it's not him in particular. He's the one who left me alone again tonight.

I don't understand this about him. Our entire marriage has been this way. We rarely ever fight and get along like the best of friends and partners. When we do have sex, as soon as it's over, my husband is back to working in his office, or winding down, as he calls it. He then falls asleep on the couch after eating and watching a few hours of television. I guess I shouldn't complain. I just think that there are couples who have been married for years like us who do sleep in the same bed and have a fantastic sex life. I would love to experiment and reignite that passion. I honestly don't know how to bring the subject up or if he would be receptive. He is always working or preoccupied with something other than me. I sometimes feel like I'm a roommate. He takes it for granted that I will always be here, waiting. So, here I am, another night, staring at the ceiling.

My phone buzzes on the nightstand. It's an email from Andrew. Right away, I notice it's a private account, not a military account. My stomach twists a bit as I open the email not knowing what to anticipate.

Dear Grace,

I hope my email finds you well. I am glad you were willing for us to know more about one another. I was impressed reading your background and work ethic. A strong work ethic is something I value having been in the military for 36 years now. Here's a bit about me: I am 58 years old, divorced now for 10 years and have one son. I am an officer in the US Air Force, currently deployed to Afghanistan. I enjoy reading, experiencing excellent food and wine, and travel. Just by your photo and reading your background, I am going to venture a guess that you and I are very much alike.

My parents immigrated to the United States from the Republic of Ireland when I was a young child. My father was a minister and my mother stayed home to care for me. I was their only child when tragically, they were killed in a car accident when I was six years old. I was taken in by a Catholic charity for orphans until I was old enough to leave and be on my own. Don't feel sorry for me about this Grace. I only tell you, so you know my background. My life has made me a survivor, and I am where I am today because of my determination. There was no one to catch me if I fell. So, I decided never to fall.

Neither of my parents had siblings to my knowledge and my grand-parents were already dead when my parents moved to the US. I have no family left other than my son. I want to start over when I am out of this place. I want another chance at a happy family whether that's more of my own children or someday, grandchildren. I want to gather them up at bedtime and read stories to them until their little eyes close. I want that life. I would love to have a beautiful wife to share it with me.

Physically, I am 6'2 and about 200 pounds. I exercise daily, mostly push-ups and strength training with my boys. I need to be honest with you, I am ready at this point in my life to find my soul mate. I will be returning to the US soon. My career in the military is nearly finished and I am ready to start a new chapter in my life. I would like to find someone to share my time with and someone who can build a great life with me. I am not ready for retirement, but want to start a new business, probably in cybersecurity. No pressure, Grace, I just want to be transparent with you. A new friendship is always welcome, don't you think?

I look forward to learning more about you and will anticipate an email from you soon.

Fondly,

Andrew

While I was reading, something in me decided to write him back. He seems successful and driven. I like interacting with other professionals who have determination and purpose like him. There is nothing wrong with a new friendship. That's always welcome, just like he said. I will be honest though and lay all my cards on the table, that I am married. If this stops here, I'll be ok with that. If it doesn't, well, I'll know that I was honest with him.

I start writing, hoping my husband isn't still awake and sees my bedroom light on.

Dear Andrew,

Thank you for sharing more about who you are. I need to be honest up front. I am married. I agree and think there's no harm in emailing, but I understand if you don't want to talk to me now.

I am 43 years old, have 3 beautiful, wonderful children, all teenagers. I live a quiet life by most standards. I love to cook, especially trying new recipes. I love to garden and read. I am currently reading a biography about a blind man who climbed Mt. Everest. The power of the human spirit is amazing, don't you think? Of course, being a military officer, you probably have seen countless examples of such resilience.

My parents are still alive. My mother was recently diagnosed with breast cancer and is undergoing treatment. I am making frequent weekend trips to their home to check on her and my dad. I have one sister living in New York.

I work long hours for my company, often bringing my work home. I try to keep family a priority though, so that sometimes means I am logged on long after everyone else is asleep. I find my work interesting and worthwhile. It is exciting to me to manage the resources that make the work happen. I also teach a class at a private university. The classes are all online and that comes with its own challenges. I enjoy my students. I think they appreciate the real-world examples and stories that I weave into the subject matter. Teaching is something I would like to continue to do for as long as I can. I feel like I learn something new each semester.

How old is your son? I suppose he lives with his mother while you are deployed? Do you get to speak with him often? Being separated from him must be so hard, I cannot imagine the sacrifice you have made.

What do you do to relax? Do you enjoy sports? Will you share what it is like to be a pilot? I love to fly when I travel, I can only imagine what flying a fighter jet must be like.

Hope you have a pleasant evening...actually, what time is it there?
My best,
Grace

I can't sleep at all. I am overthinking this. I feel a little guilty that I am emailing another man, but honestly, it's nice to get some attention especially from a successful man. A girl needs to feel like she is interesting and attractive, right? Am I playing with fire? Of course not, it's just an email, that's all. This is crazy, like always, I'm overthinking this. I'm not going to give another thought to this man and just get some sleep.

Chapter 4

At 5:00 am, my phone buzzes on the nightstand. It's him…. okay, maybe I'm not overthinking this….

Dear Grace,

Thank you for sharing a bit more. I must tell you that your email was like a cool breeze in this desert. First, to answer your questions, my son is 17 and enrolled in a university in London, studying economics. I don't get to see him often or talk on the phone much, but we do exchange emails often. His mother has remarried, and I don't really know exactly where she is. It was not a pleasant divorce. I would have liked to have had more children, but they don't exactly appear where there is only fighting. I wanted to surprise her one day by coming home early. I was the one who was shocked. That is in the past now, so enough about that.

I was able to attend college on scholarships and hard work. I joined the Air Force after getting my degree. I have been immersed in military life ever since. I have traveled many places in the world because of my military service but have traveled a bit for pleasure as well. Hawaii is one of my favorite places. I also enjoyed Bali, although I was only there for a brief leave between assignments. The oceans seem to heal me and bring me back to life.

Flying is like nothing else, Grace. I feel completely alive when I am in the air. We train constantly and it never gets old for me. Of course, we must know how to parachute as well. Would you ever step out into the air with nothing beneath your feet? I would love to teach you someday. Tell me, are you much of a risk taker?

I enjoy sports, especially football, but not the American kind. I golf and stay active when I am not working, which is rare, especially now. I love to read just like you do. I have some suggestions for you if you are interested. You seem to work nonstop, and these books will help you to find balance and meaning. Meditation and focus are very important, Grace. You can't just hit the ground running each morning; it will wear you down.

I keep looking at your profile picture. Is it recent? You are a very beautiful woman. Describe your appearance to me more in your next email if you would be so kind. I would like us to talk more, would you?

Affectionately,

Andrew

He didn't even acknowledge that I shared I was married. So, does that mean it didn't bother him? Interesting, I will mention it again and see how he reacts. He has guessed correctly about me, I do immerse myself in work, sometimes without any break on the weekend or evening. How did he know that? And what books will he suggest?

I start composing another email to him, mentioning again my husband and children. This time blatantly so it's plainly there if he wants to bow out of this developing friendship. I tell him I'd like to keep our emails private as I don't think my husband would approve. I hope he will understand that this is just a friendship. I move on to ask what books he suggests for me. I ask if he has an Irish accent, which I think is sexy, but I don't share that. I tell him the profile picture is from a few years earlier, but I basically look the same, but a few more laugh lines. I describe myself as having blonde hair, a curvy body, average height, though people often describe me as tall since I wear heels most days. I ask for a recent picture of him. I ramble on about my job and ask a few more questions. I end the email and get ready for work.

By the time I arrive at work, he has emailed me back. I googled the time difference and found it's 11 and a half hours. A quick thought runs through my mind that for an officer deployed in a war zone, he seems to have adequate time for personal correspondence. This email is a bit more direct. He acknowledges my marriage, but states that shouldn't stop us from talking. He shares the titles and authors of five books he would like me to consider. Two are about inner focus and being in the moment, one about the American education system, and two about spiritual awakening. He suggests we should be able to talk more frequently, possibly on a messaging app. He shares more details about what he hopes to accomplish when he finishes his current assignment. I feel as if he is subtly placing me into those plans, without directly saying it. He ends by telling me how special my emails are, and that he is looking forward to them more and more. Before closing, he again suggests a messaging app so we can quickly chat whenever we like.

So now what do I do? Like I can start chatting with someone like I'm a teenager? I am a professional with a demanding job and a family, I can't do this. I don't have time for myself, let alone for this new relationship. But there is something about him….and wow, he intrigues me. I have always found military men sexy, and his profile photo is the picture of a successful man, the total package. We have so much in common. In my email response, I avoid his suggestion to move to a messaging app. Thankfully he doesn't bring it up again when he replies later.

I think back to when I awoke to Andrew's message this morning. I was all alone in that king-size bed and wearing a silk nightie that I purchased on my birthday. How pathetic is that? A woman buying her own lingerie…. I suddenly feel very alone. I'm certainly haven't heard my husband wanting to discuss any books or anything else with me for that matter. I pause, thinking about that fact, and go online and order all five of the books Andrew suggested I read.

CHAPTER 5

A few weeks pass and our emails become more detailed and personal. Since we started talking, I am beginning to look forward to hearing from him. He makes me feel attractive, interesting, and desired. I forgot the incredible feeling of a new relationship.

Sometimes, as I read his emails again, I think of flirty things to say when I write back. I start to think more about my clothes, my health, and my appearance. What would he like to see? I always took great care to look polished since in my business I am expected to represent the company as a professional. That includes staying fit and looking the part. However, I admitted to Andrew my profile picture is from a few years earlier. I know there are a few laugh lines around my eyes and maybe a few extra pounds on my hips. I will step up my game and take better care of myself. I'll do it for me though, not for him. I've made up my mind and absolutely want to continue talking with Andrew. I can take care of myself and decide who I should talk to, even though I'm married.

I decide to find a secure messaging app. I do a little research, avoiding the apps that got bad reviews or have had security problems. I see a few articles that warn against common methods that scammers use with these apps. I read through the details of each quickly and find one that looks safe. I must be careful for both of us since Andrew is in another country. I set up an account and be sure I can lock it out when I'm not on it. I email him my contact information for the app.

Within minutes, he responded, telling me how happy he is that I want to talk and keep him company. I find myself talking even more freely and so does he. We talk for hours off and on every day, often at random times. Sometimes, he wakes me up in the middle of the night. Sometimes, he writes to me when, if I have calculated the time difference correctly, he should be sleeping. Many days, we will chat while I am at the office. I am always careful to turn off the notifications when I am home with my family. But, later, when I lay down at night, I will see messages waiting.

CHAPTER 6

I feel like Andrew is being open and honest with me and I love this new relationship we are building. But sometimes I have a funny feeling about him. There are a few questions he seems to avoid, like how long he's been deployed or when he thinks he will be returning home. He says he can't focus on that because it causes stress and he starts to feel hopeless. He tells me the key to survival and sanity for all these years in the military is to live in the now. He encourages me to read the books he suggested to learn about techniques to be present in the moment and manage stress. He insists that will help me in my demanding position at work. After we have been chatting for a couple of months, he finally shares that he's been in Afghanistan for 3 years and elsewhere in the Middle East before that. But he asks me to forgive him for not wanting to share more than that. He says what is in the past needs to stay there. I tell him I respect his wishes.

He also avoids talking about his home in Florida or provides very vague details. I ask what the layout of the house is like, and he acts as though he does not understand what I mean. I finally get him to understand I was just asking about the number of bedrooms, bathrooms, how many stories, etc. He brushes it off, and tells me that is something that only women are interested in. He would rather talk about cars. He says he owns some very fast, expensive cars. We laugh when I say he must always like to feel like he's flying.

On other topics, he is very open. He tells me he enjoys horseback riding. This was an activity I enjoyed when I was younger but haven't done in many years. He talks about his friend's home in Florida where he rides when he is at home. He is enthusiastic about the care of horses and everything he says is just how I remember it too. He is thrilled that I would like to start that hobby again. We make a promise to ride together someday.

I have noticed that sometimes, in our chat, he misspells words or uses phrases that are unusual to me. One day he said, "Am having a headache." And another, "I wan go to that place." His emails are very long and composed so I justify the texting errors because of trying to respond quickly. On the other hand, the chat seems to have allowed him to get more open with his feelings and honestly, I am starting to feel the same. I am very hesitant to reveal my feelings or even admit them to myself. It scares me to think of ever leaving my marriage. I love my husband and children so much. I have no doubt that my husband is faithful to me even though he isn't attentive. He provides for us; we don't ever argue; maybe he is just content with what our marriage has become. At least I don't think I should doubt him, but does anyone ever really know? I guess my question is: What have we become? Just friends? Roommates? Partners? Whatever it is, he does not make me feel the way Andrew has. Andrew makes me feel wanted and desired, not just in a physical way, but for my intellect and to share ideas.

He tells me often how beautiful and intelligent I am. He gets excited when I share something great my children did or a success I had at work. He doesn't share many details about his position, but when he does, I feel proud and happy. It seems that we are connected somehow, even though we have never met in person. I can almost sense when he is having a bad day, even before we have talked. Then later when he is telling me what happened, I am amazed at how I feel so in tune to his emotions. He is different than any man I know. Andrew won't admit this, but he is emotional. At times, he seems on top of the world, and others, like there is no hope. I wish I could comfort him on the bad days.

CHAPTER 7

It's finally spring. I'm so glad because this winter has been brutal. Just like the small-town neighbors I grew up with, I find myself telling Andrew the weather forecast. It's been cold, bitter, freezing, and any other adjective for cold. And it's lasted for months and months. He laughs and say that's exactly why one should live in Florida. He has no desire to be anywhere cold.

"Do you have any idea when you will be able to return home?" I ask again, knowing he probably won't know.

"They are saying that I have just a couple of months left here," he replies.

"Wow, that's great. You finally have an idea at least," I say.

"I can't wait to see you. Do you want to start making plans?" he asks me.

My heart feels like it stopped. What do I say? How would I be able to see him without my family knowing?

"Ahh, your silence tells on you, Grace. Did you not ever have any intention of meeting me in person? Are your feelings not real?" His reply has a mocking, defensive edge.

"Yes, my feelings are real. I just need a minute to think. When I asked you before when you were coming home, you never knew. I didn't expect that you would have an answer. Especially one so soon," I quickly type back.

"The first person I want to see is you, Grace. We will fly into DC and have meetings for a few days. Do you think you could meet me at the airport to welcome me home?"

"I don't know, honestly. What would I tell my family?"

"I guess you need to think about that," he answers.

"Andrew, I care about you very much. To be honest, I am very scared to meet you. What if you don't like what you see? What if I don't?

19

You haven't sent me any recent pictures of you. I can't imagine traveling to a city to see a man I've never met."

"Grace, you have no reason to worry. You have met me; I've revealed as much as I can to you about myself. You know that security is a priority here and, in my position, I can't risk anything. I will see what I can do about a picture if you insist. I know it's important to you. And you don't have to worry that I won't like what I see. I will love setting my eyes on you for the first time and I will never take them off you. You are beautiful. More importantly, you are beautiful on the inside. I love everything about you," he answers. "I have every intention to be close to you. I won't push you to leave your husband. But I think you will know what to do when the time comes. Are you reading the books I suggested, Grace? You must learn to be true to yourself. You have to really decide what it is you want for your life. Don't look back and regret that you were scared to accept happiness."

"I love what we have. But I need time. I need to take this slowly. I can't hurt my husband or my children. But I don't want to lose you."

"I won't push you, Grace. I won't interfere or make things hard for you. But someday, if I must, I will fight for you. I will fight for you, but I won't beg for your love. And I won't accept second place in your life."

I say that I understand, appreciate his patience and that we need time to see how this goes. When I remind him that I have said from the very beginning that I have no intention of jeopardizing my marriage, he gets quiet and says he is being summoned away. He states he'll be busy and doesn't know when he can write again.

CHAPTER 8

A long week passes without any messages from Andrew. My family and I travel to see my mother. She is right in the middle of her chemotherapy and very sick. I try to give my dad a break for a while, but he doesn't want to leave her. She looks like a ghost. She is like a shell of the vibrant, active woman she always was. I can hardly look into her eyes without crying. I help her with her medicine, and later with her bath. Her hair is gone, and her fair complexion is almost translucent. I've always heard about how the parent child relationship changes and eventually the child takes care of the parent. I never thought that would happen to my mom. She is the pillar that holds our family up in hard times. I am having a very hard time seeing her this way.

After her bath, I settle her into her bed. Dad is in family room talking with my husband and the kids. I hear them laughing and smile.

"It's so good to have you here, Grace. And so good to hear the laughter from the family," my mother says softly. "Hop up here on the bed with me."

I recline next to her. Her bed is just like I remember when I was little. This is the most comforting place in the world to me. I feel some tears start to run down my cheek.

"So, tell me what is going with you, Grace. You look tormented this weekend. I know it's more than just seeing me like this."

How do mothers do that? It's like this magical thing, I swear they can see into your soul. I know because I can do it to my own kids. Mothers always know when something is wrong. I remember once, my sister got in trouble when she was a small child. She asked Mom how she knew what she had done, because she wasn't in the room to see her misbehave. Mom told her that mothers have eyes on the back of their heads so they can always see their children. Later, that evening, after all was forgiven, my sister was standing on the couch next to my mother, playing with her hair.

"What are you doing, Claire?" my mom asked her.

"I am trying to find the eyes in the back of your head, Mommy," she answered.

Mother just laughed and said that children can't see them, they are just there. I honestly don't know how old we were when we finally realized she was teasing us.

"Grace? Look at me. What is it? I can tell something is wrong," my mother asked again.

"Oh nothing, the usual, I guess. Work and the family are as busy as ever. Sometimes it's just a lot to manage. I know I'm tired and just never get a break." I can't share any more details than this with my mother. She doesn't need anything else to worry about right now. And certainly not that my marriage has become cold, and I don't know if it has a future.

My parents have been married since dad was 22 and mom was 18. I'm sure they had disagreements, but they still look at each other like teenagers in love. I don't even know if she would understand what I am going through with my husband. But I know she would not approve of my talking with Andrew.

"Grace, women are complex beings. We overthink and analyze every-thing. That's why you are so good at your job. You contemplate every possible scenario in your life. Men are not that way. They take life as it comes. They want one thing. Your attention. It doesn't matter that you have no energy left at the end of the day. They want to be with you. It's up to you to tell a man what you need. And he will probably do whatever it is.

I'm not just talking about sex and not just about your husband, Grace. And don't blush, I know what I'm talking about. You must speak up for yourself. Whoever is making you feel the way your face says you feel, needs to know what is going on in that mind of yours."

My mom wrapped her slender arm around me and pulled me close. I could smell her bath oil, the same scent she had worn as long as I can remember.

"I love you, Grace. Don't worry so much. Just be true to your heart."

Why do mothers just know?

CHAPTER 9

The weekend is over, and we are back to work and school. On Tuesday, Andrew finally messages me back with vague reasons for the absence. I ask questions, but he says there are some things he can't tell me. Andrew is clearly upset by whatever happened and I keep pushing for him to confide in me. Finally, he tells me he lost a friend there the day before and is planning for transportation of his remains back to the US and a funeral.

"Why do you have to do that? I thought the military arranges that," I ask.

He becomes angry that I would question him since I haven't been in the military and certainly not in his situation. As he is ranting about the situation and my lack of understanding, I notice his words and phrases change. He communication evolves such that it isn't how an American would speak. One thing that stands out is that he types Am instead of I'm. At first, I thought it was a typo, but he keeps doing it. I keep quiet though and observe. This isn't the time to ask him about it and I don't want to upset him further.

He unloads his grief and frustration for almost an hour. Since I'm in my office, I just keep working and when his next message pops up, I offer what I hope is an appropriate sentiment. He doesn't acknowledge my message and just continues texting, pouring out his grief and anger. After each message, I tell him I am so sorry that he lost his friend and anything else I can to try to comfort him. Ignoring most of my comments, he continues about his friend, the military, and Afghanistan; it seems he is really upset about everything, not just his friend's death. I try getting him to reminisce about the good times he had with his friend, hoping that might help. I ask him what his friend was like, was he married, what his job was there, but suddenly he says he doesn't want to talk about him. I don't know what else to say to express my sympathy without it seeming flippant especially since we are just using the chat.

Oddly, his mood quickly changes for the better and he asks me how I feel about him and if I trust him. I answer honestly that I love getting to know more about him. My response doesn't seem to be what he is seeking.

"What can I do to help you feel closer to me? I am sharing feelings with you, Grace and I don't do that with anyone, ever. I can't, not in my position. I feel so close to you, but I think you have a wall around you, and you don't want to let me in. I am here serving our country and you seem to question me about many things," he tells me.

I stare at my phone feeling defeated. That comment doesn't set well with me after I have been listening to him for over an hour.

"What do you mean? I love talking with you. You are right, I don't understand how much pressure and stress you endure every day," I say.

"Do you trust me?" he asks.

"You have never given me a reason not to trust you," I reply.

"Good, trust is so important to me, Grace. If I can't trust one of my boys, do you think I want them with us here, in this place? Trust is all we have here, my love. It's all we have in life. I am going to be bold with you. I feel like I'm falling for you, Grace. You are a perfect complement to me. You are always a lady; you sense my emotions and know just what to say to help me in this terrible place. You calm me. You have a presence, like a queen. I'd really like another photo of you, I need to see you before I go to sleep at night. Something to make me smile," he says.

I pause, too long, I guess… I see that he is typing.

"You don't have to answer back about your feelings, not yet. I know this is moving fast. But when I feel something so strong, I can't sit here quietly. Take your time, my love. And if you don't feel the same, it won't change us. I will still be here, your friend, your lover, whatever you want me to be. Whatever you need. I know your family situation complicates this. I won't intrude. I will fight someday for you if that is what it takes. But I will not make anything difficult for you. We will stand the test of time. Just wait and trust me, Grace. Regarding the picture, forgive me. I know I was bold to ask you. I understand if you won't send me anything. But if it makes you more comfortable, I would like to send you a picture of me. But we aren't allowed to have cameras as officers, but I could see what I can do."

Is that true, he can't have a camera, I wonder? Maybe, it is. I convince myself that due to security, that is likely true.

I write back, "I'll see what I can do."

Andrew seems more like himself again. He says he has a dog, a German Shepard named Sarge. We talk about music and he sends me a few links to some artists that he thinks I would like. As usual, he guessed correctly. Also sending me some I had never heard of, but I was instantly drawn into the music. I am amazed at how he can figure out so quickly what my likes and dislikes are. He tells me his favorite food, which is some type of Mexican fish that I have never heard of. He talks about all the places he has travelled and where he thinks I would enjoy. He suggests a few more books for me to read that have helped him in his career and to manage a healthy mental balance. I really enjoy our time together when he is like this. I feel closer and closer to him each day. We continue talking off and on the rest of the day about our likes and dislikes, until it's way past the time I should be asleep. I must get some rest. We say goodnight.

CHAPTER 10

Almost every morning, I awake to a message or an email from him.

Dear Grace,

I have a big conference starting this week and will be working long hours. I'm not sure how often we will get to talk this week. Have I told you today that you are so beautiful and such a wonderful mother? I would love to hear more about you and your children. It makes me so sad to think I missed a chance for you to be my wife. Life has cheated us, and I am 20 years too late. I dream about you and think how your body is so beautiful, especially next to me, in my arms. I just want to look at you, stare into your eyes, just appreciate the woman God planned for me.

My favorite color is turquoise, the color of the ocean. My home in Florida is very near the beach. I meditate and find peace there whenever I need to retreat. Do you enjoy the ocean, Grace? It reminds me of your beautiful blue eyes. I would be happy just to drown in them as we hold one another. I want your body wrapped around me every night, as we lay in bed and talk about our dreams and our future. I would love to have another child, but only with you as my beautiful wife. A little girl, life would be complete then. You would never have to worry, and I would take care of you every single day.

I won't be able to write often this week, but I would love to come back to my room late to find an email waiting for me. Just know that someone in a faraway desert is dreaming of you.

Love and affection,

Andrew

Andrews often includes a couple of links to some love songs at the end of his emails. I listen to each song over and over. Wow, I think, he is serious. I feel my heart beginning to ache for him already since I know I won't hear from him much this week at all. I want to give him the time he needs for his important conference, so I decide not to message, at least not right away. I'll just try to get back to life as usual.

The children have a busy week with school and sports so that helps to pass the time. My mind keeps wandering though. I miss talking to him so much. I occasionally check our chat and I can see the last time he was online. I smile when I think that like me, he goes back to it and reads our messages again. It appears he does this often, almost as if he is studying our communication. I pour myself into some work projects and try to stay focused. The weather has gotten so cold here again. I was wrong when I said spring had arrived. The skies are gray and low, much like my mood. It's that time of year that nice weather is just a tease. A glimpse of warm, spring weather and then the cold comes back and settles in my bones colder than before. There is no joy or anticipation of spring, just cold, damp weather.

On Wednesday, I decide to leave the office early. I'm sick of this weather, everything is grey and freezing cold. I decide I'm going shopping. Some retail therapy is in order, that will help my mood. I spend most of the afternoon browsing, trying pieces on, deciding against them, and just wandering through the stores. Finally, still wandering, I take the escalator up and find the lingerie department. There it is, something sexy and delicate, just what I need. A lacy sheer bra and cheeky panties to match. The mannequin is displayed in them in black with pink trim. They are gorgeous and I have to get them. I look through racks quickly to find my size and find that they also have them in turquoise. It's even more beautiful, a turquoise with just a bit of a sand colored trim. My mind flashes back to Andrew. He said turquoise is his favorite color, it reminds him of the beach. In the dead of winter, I couldn't find anything more perfect. Without even glancing at the price, I take it to the register, and they are mine.

My mood is lighter, optimistic. I know this will make him happy. How can I show him? I have never taken any intimate pictures of myself. I feel awkward and unattractive just thinking about it. Ok, Grace, get that out of your head, I tell myself. I want to do this for him. This will show him exactly how I feel. I'm going to do it, just as soon as I have the house to myself. I feel naughty, exhilarated and but very determined.

CHAPTER 11

When I arrive home, I shove the bag into the bottom of my purse. This set isn't for my husband to see, ever. Only Andrew. He is my secret. Yes, my secret. The more I think about that, the more it turns me on. I haven't felt this way in a very long time. The newness of us, each day a new thought or discovery about one another. I cannot wait to see his reaction.

I go through the evening cooking dinner, cleaning, helping with homework and answering email. By 10 pm, I am more than ready to call it a day. The kids are in their rooms, on their phones with friends, and finished with their homework. I sit in the living room, waiting for my husband to look up from his work or away from the tv. Fifteen minutes pass. What a waste of my time. I speak up, telling him I think I will go to bed now. Just a slight acknowledgment, nothing more. I think, oh well, I have something and someone to keep me busy anyway.

I head to my bedroom and undress for my shower. The hot water feels amazing on my skin and sore muscles. Running my hands over my wet, soapy body, I secretly wish it was Andrew's hands all over me. I think about his picture, his smile, and his peppery grey hair. I imagine what his body looks like and I feel a shudder run through me. He is so distinguished and handsome. I know he will be a gentle, experienced lover. My fantasy starts, and he is watching me in the shower, smiling at me, then asking to join me. I smile back and my answer is to slide the glass door open so he can enter.

He is behind me now, running his strong hands all over my wet, soapy body. I moan softly, then remember where I am, and try to be quiet. I can almost feel his body pressed firm against my back and hips. "Please, I want you so much, just take me," the thought keeps running through my mind. I envision him entering me from behind and making love to me, as the water pours on our bodies. It is so wonderful. So wonderful to be in his arms, nothing else matters now. The thought of him making love to me takes me to the edge. I hold myself against the tiles of the shower until my body stops and I can catch my breath. My release is incredible; I can only imagine what it will be like when we meet.

I finish my shower, lightheaded and glowing. After toweling off my body and hair, I wrap up with my robe. This is the perfect opportunity to try to take a picture for him. I apply a little makeup and finish drying my hair. He has only one picture of me and in it my hair is styled straight in my boring professional cut. I want to let my natural curls happen for this one. I do a little bit of styling to put them in place and am satisfied with how it looks. I apply a wonderfully scented body oil all over my skin next, then finish with some perfume. Laughing to myself, I wonder why I'm putting on perfume for this, but it seems to help set the mood.

I suddenly feel very guilty. What the hell am I doing? I'm married, I can't seriously be considering taking a picture like this, can I? Wrapping my robe around me, I decide I should see what my husband is doing.

"Baby?" I call down the hall to his office.

He barely looks up. "What are you doing up, Grace? You have to work tomorrow; you need to get to sleep."

"I just wondered if you were coming to bed," I ask.

"You know I have work to do, why would you ask me that?"

"Yes, I know. I just thought you might be finished," I reply.

"You better get to bed," he doesn't even look up at me, just keeps looking at his computer and the papers in front of him.

"Ok, good night," I say.

No response as I walk away, down the hallway to my room. Well, I tried, but got nothing. More of the same reasons, too busy to pay any attention to me at all. I am more determined than I was earlier to make this picture for Andrew. I want it to be perfect. I know I am attractive, and at least Andrew appreciates me. Now he'll have something special to keep him warm at night.

In my room, I pull the tags off my purchase and lay them on the bed. They really are beautiful. The cut of the leg on the panties comes up in the back to outline my hips. The bra is sheer in just the right places. I slip the panties on and they fit perfectly. Now for the bra. I slide it over my arms and hook it in the back. I adjust the cups around my breasts. They spill over the top slightly, just enough. I turn and look at myself in the mirror. I don't feel or look like an exhausted 43-year-old, full time executive, and mother of 3 teenagers. I feel sexy. I almost don't recognize the girl looking back at me. But I'm there, that person is really who I am. I'm alive again, this moment I am in right now, is the most real and connected I've been in a long time. No more going through the motions. I am going to make my life count for me. Yes, I'll still be a wife, a great mother, and a hard-working professional woman. But my eyes will be wide open from now on. Thank you, Andrew. I thank you for bringing me back to life.

Okay, deep breath and down to this picture business. I look at my bedspread. Nice, but not a sexy backdrop. Hopefully, he won't notice anything else but me in the picture though, I smile to myself. I move the bedspread around a bit to make it look a little more inviting. Did I really just think inviting, my bed and him all in the same thought??

I have my phone and tap the camera, turning it to selfie mode. I am trying to think how to do this without dropping the phone on my face. Good grief, how do teenagers take selfies all day? This is complicated and they make it look so easy. Of course, they aren't working with 43-year-old subject matter. I lay back and bring one leg up on the bed, so my hips are tilted slightly. I check the camera and think I like what I see. I snap the picture. Ugh, I was making a face like I am concentrating really hard. Which I am, but he doesn't need to know that. Ok, take 2. About 10 pictures later, I have one I like. It's not magazine centerfold quality but not too bad. I look good. I have a bit of the "come hither" look I was going for, and the lingerie looks great. At this moment, I am so thankful I've put myself through the torture of running almost every day since my children were born.

Ok, I need to take a moment and breathe before I send anything. I change into some shorts and a tank top for bed. I put the new bra and panties in my drawer for safe keeping. I hop into bed and pull up the photos on my phone. Maybe a little editing? A crop here and there and a filter to bring out the color of the bra and panties. As I do that, I notice it enhances my eyes too. Well, Andrew likes my eyes, so I'll take that as a bonus. It can't hurt my chances anyway.

I decide to send the picture in the messaging app and just say something like "I'm thinking of you". Let the picture do the talking, right? I'm nervous, but I am ready to show him that I care. I hit send, no going back now. All I can do is wait. I doubt I'm going to sleep much but I will try. I curl up with a book but keep having to read numerous pages twice because my mind keeps wandering to imagine what he will say. Finally, and thankfully, sleep overtakes me, and I get some much-needed rest.

In the early morning hours, my phone alerts me. I wake with a start, thinking it can't be time to get ready for work already. The time flashes 4:30 am. Not quite time to get up. I lay my head back on the pillow, then I remember what I did last night and grab my phone. It's him. My heart is pounding while I struggle to open my sleepy eyes enough to unlock the app we use.

"Wow, oh my God, you are so gorgeous," his message starts. "I hope everyone in your life appreciates how beautiful and amazing you are. You are the most beautiful woman I have ever laid my eyes on. Grace, my beautiful Grace. I love this, so much. Thank you, my darling, thank you. You have no idea what this means to me. You are my treasure, my love. I am going to say it and I hope it doesn't scare you, I can't stop thinking about you. I'm afraid that I am falling in love with you and we haven't even met. I know God has a plan for us, Grace. Please understand that. We found each other for a reason."

I am so happy after reading his message. Yes, I agree…. We haven't even met, but we have so much in common and I feel so connected, so in love. I am falling for him. I know I am. I have no regrets about it either. It just feels so right. I lay back down and spend the hour I have left before the alarm goes off thinking of him.

CHAPTER 12

My morning starts out as usual when I get to the office. My secretary, Sophia and I work through the day's agenda, voice mail and other correspondence that needs attention. She then leaves me to spreadsheets and working on budget projections as our fiscal year is about to end. About mid-morning, I decide to take a break and grab some coffee. It seems the team all had a good weekend, and everyone is in a cheerful mood, me included. I take my coffee back to my office and shut the door. In a few minutes, I have written Andrew, asking about the conference and what progress has been made regarding his friend's funeral arrangements. I again express my sympathies for that terrible loss. I can't help but think how strange that situation seems. He said his friend is an American but no longer serving, he just had some unfinished business before departing for home. I wonder how it was that he was killed in an attack if he isn't active duty. I decide to do a web search for any news of an American killed recently in Afghanistan. Nothing recent. Of course, maybe they don't release information right away. I don't know, it just seems strange that the government wouldn't immediately take action to return his body home to his family. I upset Andrew the first time I questioned him about that, so I will just wait and see. Surely, there will be news about it in a few days.

I ask about his son and his studies. It's so strange that he says he doesn't know where his ex-wife is now. I could see that if they didn't have a child together, but I can't imagine how divorced parents wouldn't have to communicate at least occasionally. I inquire if he has heard any more news about returning home. Before closing, I share a few things that I have done with my girls and Seth lately.

I feel uneasy, like something is off. I am still thinking about how odd that situation with his friend is. I do another web search to try to find any pictures of Andrew. Since he is a military officer, there must be some press releases that include a picture or quote from him. I search specifically for the Air Force and come up with nothing. I remove Air Force from the search bar and hit enter again. A few men with the same name, but none of their profiles or information match anything close. I frown. In the world today, a web search will find at least something on just about anyone. Whether it's true or not is another thing, but at least an address or social media profile. I try a search for his name and the town in Florida that he calls home. Again, nothing. I am starting to feel very suspicious. I'll have to think about how to ask him about this. Maybe he can send me a picture or some proof of his existence. My mind is racing, but I must get back to work, I can't think about this now.

I didn't hear from him until 4 am the next morning when my phone buzzes on the nightstand. Again, I'm alone in this king size bed my husband and I are supposed to share. I frown and roll my eyes as I reach for my phone. It's not a message, but an email.

Dear Grace,

My main purpose for writing you this message is to tell you how special you are making me feel now as far as this communication is concerned. My heart is turning inside me, and I can feel you close to me even though many miles separate us. I'm grateful that I found you and you care enough to make such an effort in your communications with me. You are a very special person and you will be in my life forever. I think of all the ways you make my life complete, and I ran out of space when I tried to fit it on just one sheet. I love to imagine you and me forever, I love to imagine ways to always make our relationship better. I love to imagine how we will make up after having a fight.

I love to imagine how you are going to react after you read this letter. I want you to feel as special as I do, so I will tell you that I will do all in my power to care for you, support you, and be there for you. I will dream of feeling your arms around me holding me very close and I will hold you just as close, and I will kiss you and feel your skin close to mine...And when you are sad I will make you smile, and when you are happy, I will share your joy. And I will support you and stand by you and make sure the world knows how special you by staying by your side and holding your hand through life's problems.

Every day, I find something new in you; something that makes me feel different but sure in one thing—you are something more, something deeper. I am sending you this letter to share with you some of the things that I want to do with you in the future and how I am going to make you happy at some point in this lifetime:

I want to be your best friend.
Spend the rest of my life with you.
Dance with you in the rain
Stargaze on a clear night with you
Watch the sunset together with you
Spend all day with you doing nothing
I want to be more proud of you than I already am at this very moment
Go on a carriage ride through the park with you
Go to brunch with you
Go for a twilight horseback ride with you
Watch a bad movie together with you
Have our picture taken together
Eat ice cream with you
Open the door for you
Go to a museum together with you
Talk to you using only body language
Give you space when you need it
Accept you totally and completely—flaws and all
Discuss current events in a heated debate with you
Carve our names into a tree/table
Go for a walk a dusk together
Spend all night thinking of 101 sweet things to do for you
Hold you and gaze into your eyes and realize how much I love you….and tell you
Gently run my hand across your cheek and look into your eyes
Blindfold you and take you somewhere romantic
Spend my life making you feel your heartbeat
Give you a backrub when you need it
Always being honest with you

*Have our first fight, make up and feel a stronger bond because
we very successfully
weathered the storm—together
Laugh at something with you
Share a plate of spaghetti with you
Give you an unexpected surprise on special occasions
Go on a road trip across Europe and Asia with you
Count thunderclaps together with you during a storm
Envelop you in my soul
Cook your favorite meal
Know you better than you know yourself
Plant a tree in our yard together
Look over at you during a party and you know without me saying
a word –that I love
you
Be able to say "I love you" in 89 different languages —in 89 dif-
ferent countries
Hold you when you're at your saddest and comfort you when
you need it the most
Be the one you come to for that comfort and holding
Wipe away the day's stresses and issues with just a hug and kiss
Make love to you passionately
Grow old with you. Yes......grow old with you*

*All of the above, I would like to share with you, so I would like us
to give this relationship a chance to grow and see what comes out of it
because they say journey of a thousand miles begins with just one step.
I will stop here for now but hope you enjoy the rest of your day wherever
you may be now…I hope you are not offended by me being straightfor-
ward with you, I'm just asking you to keep it real and be honest with
your feelings; and this way you know where I stand.
Yours affectionately,
Officer Andrew*

Good lord, I had to read that twice. That was a lot of emotion, but
I have to say this really doesn't feel right. It doesn't sound like Andrew,
I am ashamed to have this thought, but I am thinking it sounds like
someone else wrote it. It just doesn't sound like something a military

officer would write to a woman. I know he is busy this week, but would he have someone else write something or find a love letter online just to check the box that he wrote to me? My mind keeps going back to my web searches and coming up with nothing. Could he be a fraud? I hope not, but…. I am an intelligent woman. I should trust my instincts. I need a picture of him, that will help me to decide. I need more information before I let my mind run with this terrible feeling I have. That is only fair to him, I shouldn't jump to conclusions.

I write him a quick note on the messaging app. I thank him for the beautiful email and say how much I appreciate the expression of emotion and that I feel the same. I ask if it would be possible to get a picture other than the social media profile picture. He had told me that it was a few years old, so I use that angle to justify wanting a more current picture and that "it will keep me warm at night" like he stated to me. I glance at the time, sighing; I have to get up now and start another busy day. I guess I'll see how he responds.

CHAPTER 13

Late in the evening, he writes me back on the app, saying that the conference has broken for a break and he walked back to the office to get some fresh air. I text back, say I am glad to hear from him and hope everything is going well. He says it should be wrapping up in the next day or so and he will see what can be done regarding the pictures. He is excited to tell me that he talked to his son yesterday. He met a wonderful girl and he wants to start a relationship with her, but he wanted his dad's advice first.

"Interesting, it must be something important he wants to ask," I write back.

"Yes, it is. He wanted to know if I thought it would be an issue if the girl he wants to date is of another nationality or another skin color," he explains.

"And what advice did you give him, Andrew?"

"What would you tell your children, Grace? Have you ever loved a black man? Or a man from another culture?"

"I believe you love who you love, Andrew. Nothing else matters. I think that is wonderful that he has found someone that he cares for and would like to know better. I haven't had a relationship with anyone out-side of my own race, but I think that should never be a concern for him or anyone else."

"Good. I like your answer, Grace, but why haven't you loved anyone outside your own race? Am just curious… you may have missed the love of your life. I told him the same, that you love who you love. I must get back now; break is surely over. I will write you when I can."

He is gone before I can even say goodbye. I am impressed. What a wonderful, supportive father he is. And it sounds like his son is a fine young man, certainly like his father. I suddenly feel bad for my doubts earlier, but still, I want to know more about this seemingly 'perfect for me' person. I can't give up until he tells me more or I can find information on my own.

I can't help myself; I download Andrew's social media profile picture since it's the only one I have and do a reverse image search. Again, nothing. That just seems so odd to me. Suddenly, I remember something he said about his home in Florida. He said he lives very near the beach. I am not familiar with the city listed on his profile, so I look it up and frown when I see where it is on the map. It is right smack in the middle of the state. Probably at least one to two hours from any beach. So, why would he tell me that he lives basically on the beach? To impress me? Or because he isn't who he claims to be? I sit back and decide to do some more research.

An hour passes and I have learned quite a bit. Typically, military personnel are deployed overseas for no more than eighteen months at a time. All travel to and from the location is coordinated and paid for by the military as well. And non-military personnel must have a pass to be on base. So, if Google hasn't let me down, none of what Andrew said about his friend's presence in Afghanistan makes any sense. I search his name and the city in Florida on his profile again. Nothing comes up other than ads for companies that charge a small fee to verify someone's identity and do a background check. I check out a few and decide to pay the small fee to dig deeper.

I enter all the information I have and then enter my credit card information. Of course, there are all kinds of add on services the company offers but I opt for the basic package. I wait for what seems like forever until the results start to appear on the screen. These companies reveal the report in an almost Hollywood way, pulling back a curtain one detail at a time, keeping the purchaser in suspense. A series of names or similar names pop up on the screen while it appears their search engines and server are doing something very top secret and dramatic for my $9.95 fee. Finally, the search is complete. And guess what, an exact match for Andrew Bronnan isn't found. How is that possible? Plenty of men with the same name, but the age or last known address doesn't match any of the information he has shared with me.

Numerous ads and other content about internet and romance scammers pop up as I search. Catfished, scammers revealed, all these headlines are flashing across the screen. I read a few and some of them say that often scammers adopt a persona of an American service member and often officers. I suddenly feel sick; I really believed him. Could this be what he is? Of course, I felt like things were moving fast on all the love stuff considering we have never seen each other in person. I really liked writing and texting with him. Am I one of those lonely, pitiful women who is an easy target? Of course, Andrew has never asked me for anything and all the webpages state that is a common theme. They have some terrible medical issue and need money sent right away, or some other urgent scenario. He has never asked me for money or anything else though. His friend's death would have provided the perfect opportunity for him if he was going to. But maybe he just hasn't yet. I'm going to trust my gut on this and get him to either confess he isn't who he says or give me more information. I need to think about how I am going to approach this, certainly by email, not the texting app. I need to sleep on this. Of course, I have nothing to distract me. I'll be alone in my bed again tonight.

CHAPTER 14

The next day, I'm in my office. It's been a long day; I've been in marketing meetings all day. We have a new drug that should get through FDA approval within weeks and everyone is eager to get it out in the market. If successful, it will benefit patients who need narcotics to control pain, but this drug is less addictive. It will also benefit our profits in a huge way. Physicians are eager for pain management options and our country is in crisis with narcotic addiction. We are doing the right thing and will be rewarded with big bonuses. But for now, I take a break and work on my email to Andrew.

Dear Andrew,

I need to speak with you about some doubts I am having about you. First, I love what is developing between us. I feel like I'm falling in love. However, I can't shake an uneasy feeling. I have to be true to not just my heart, but my intellect too. You know me, I ask a lot of questions…I need you to give me some more information about who you say you are.

You need to explain why no one by your name or birthday is on record with the military or in your city in Florida. You don't exist online at all. Just this morning, I found that your social media profile is gone. I want you to send me a picture of you, a real picture, not some stock photo. I want answers, I want to know if you are a real person.

Another thing, while your email was beautiful, it almost felt fake, like someone else wrote it. I did a web search and those words aren't yours. In fact, my search of your letter brought up information about romance scammers. Is that what you are, Andrew?

If my instinct is right, I am hurt deeply. I feel like a joke to you. That you are somewhere laughing at me. I am not a desperate, pathetic woman, Andrew. I enjoyed our new relationship and I liked you. I feel like this was all a dream. Please be honest with me. I would like answers. Grace

I feel numb. Am I so stupid to fall for someone's lies? God, I am an idiot. Please be real. I can't handle this. I have to go somewhere, do something, but I'm stuck here in my office for another couple of hours.

Later that night at home, after the kids have had dinner and are just taking it easy for the night, I go for a run. I feel like my heart is going to burst out of my chest and it's not from my running pace. I can't stop worrying that I have been a fool. How could I be so naive to think that Andrew, who I have never met, is suddenly so in love with me? How could I believe that? I am 43 and he is 58. Is that even true? Regardless, we aren't teenagers, we should know by now how relationships develop. If it's too good to be true, it probably is.

Not to forget, even though it doesn't seem like it, I'm married! God, I feel like such a jerk. I need to focus on me and really think about what is going on in my head and my heart. What happened to my marriage? Am I ready to live the rest of my life with a man who shows no affection toward his wife?

I decide I'm going to talk to my husband. Somehow, I will get his attention away from his work and really talk about our relationship. I feel like I'm going to cry as I run, just the thought of him and my children and what I might lose. I'm scared of what he will say to explain his inattention. I have never doubted him, but I'm sure thousands of women said the same before they discovered the truth. But I am talking with Andrew, that's just as bad, isn't it? Or is it?

I am literally exhausted. I realize I haven't been paying attention and have run farther than my usual route. One of the elementary schools is up ahead, I'll just sit and take a break for a few minutes and then make the long run back home. I can already tell my legs are going to make me pay for this tomorrow.

The bench is splintered and there are weeds growing up around it. The school should really do a better job of taking care of the grounds.

God knows we pay enough in our city and county taxes. This seems like a very odd place for a bench, it's not even near the playground. I dust off the portion I'm not sitting on and see a decrepit looking placard. In memory of...someone..., I can't even make out the name. How sad. Someone's family donated this in their loved one's memory, and it isn't being maintained. I think about how true that is about life. We run through our days and everything on the calendar seems so important. Then it's over and honestly, after our children are gone, does anyone really remember us? Was anything we did that important? Unless we are a world leader, or Mother Teresa, I think probably not.

I sit and try to catch my breath. Seeing the memorial on the bench reminds me of the teachings I learned in Bible class so many years ago. The greatest commandment: "Love the Lord your God with all your heart, with all your soul and with all your mind". And the second: "Love your neighbor as yourself". I remember my teacher, Mrs. Duncan (I thought she was a hundred years old; she was probably not much older than I am now) asking us, "Students, who is our neighbor?" We were young and of course, only thought of the people in our neighborhood.

"What about the people you see at your school, at the store, or your ballgames? What about the people in other states in the US? What about people on the other side of the world?"

To our little minds, we could never imagine that someone in another country was our neighbor. How is that possible? As I have gotten older, the world grew smaller. I can jump on a plane and be just about anywhere in a day's time. With technology, I can connect with someone instantly on the other side of the world.

That thought brings me back to reality. I better get home before it gets too dark. Andrew is monopolizing my thoughts as I move. Andrew, all the way on the other side of world. Just like those neighbors our teacher wanted us to consider, he is just like me, my neighbor. I just feel so connected to him, whoever he is. I want to know his truth, even if it hurts me. He is just a human and I'm not scared of discovering the truth. I wish he would write me back, so I know.

It is pitch black by the time I get to the garage door. I head upstairs and see my daughters standing in the kitchen staring at me.

"Geez, Mom, where have you been? We were just getting ready to get in the car to go look for you," Sarah says.

"I know. I just went farther than I usually do." I am still panting and getting a glass of water. "Where's your dad?"

"He is downstairs. He is in a bad mood, so we are avoiding him," they both exchange a look.

"Why is he in a bad mood?" I ask.

"When is he in a good mood?" they both shrug as they head down the hall to their rooms and important social media time.

I sigh and finish off my glass of water. They make a great point. I can't remember the last time he seemed happy to be at home. I head to my room to take a shower and collect my thoughts. Then I will try to talk to my husband or at least see how bad his mood is.

I take a quick shower and feel somewhat better, although my legs are still throbbing a bit. I better plan to wear somewhat comfortable shoes tomorrow or I will really be paying for the mini marathon I tried tonight.

I slip on some yoga pants and a tank top and pull my damp hair back. I wash my face and apply anti-aging cream just like every night. My phone is flashing on the nightstand. I hesitate, with a sinking feeling that it's Andrew. Should I look now or go have this discussion?

I decide to look. It's him. Not an email, a chat. So, whatever the response is, it will be brief. That could be good…. or very bad. I feel sick.

I open the app and see he's no longer online. His last seen at time is 8:10 pm, my time. That was about the time I was sitting on the bench at the school. I open the message, bracing for the worst.

"Grace, I know you have a curious mind, it's something I love about you. You get information and then you ask more questions. That is one of the secrets to your success. You must remember though, I told you I love you. And a relationship is between two people. Not two people and the internet. Google only contains what individuals or companies put out there, and much of the content there is false. In my position and others like me, our personal information must be kept hidden. There are many reasons for that, Grace. The most important is my safety. Our government understands that, and I hope you will too. You're correct, I did plagiarize the romantic words in my email from a website. I'm sorry I didn't quote a source; I just thought the words described accurately how I was feeling. Please ask me anything, honey. I will share what I can. I want you to know whatever you need to know about me to make you happy."

Then one more message, separate from the first: "I've attached some pictures of me, they are from an interview I did. Maybe not what you were hoping for, but it's all I have right now. I'd love some of you as well."

I sit down on the bed, smiling. He's right, I had let mind run crazy, I shouldn't have doubted him. I feel like such a jerk. I'll have to apologize. The pictures are wonderful, he's so handsome. He's talking to someone across a board room and looks commanding and brilliant. The other is in the studio for the interview. He looks just a bit older than the profile picture but even more attractive. I look at the clock and decide it's too late to have a discussion with my husband. He knows where to find me. This is his bedroom too after all.

CHAPTER 15

I awaken early to a beautiful weekend. My daughters and I have a day of shopping planned. Both have been asked to the spring formal dance, so we are on the hunt to find the perfect dress. Neither will have any issue with that. Everything they slip on looks absolutely perfect on them. They are beautiful young ladies, even if I am a bit biased.

I am in the dining room sipping my morning tea and daydreaming out the window when my husband enters.

"How did you sleep, Grace?" he stops to ask.

"Fine, and you?" I answer.

"Not bad. Are you and the girls still planning to go shopping today? I see that they are both still asleep," he says.

"Yes, but I'll let them sleep a little while longer. The dress shops won't be open this early anyway. What do you have planned for today?" I smile and ask him.

"I need to go see a client about a project, so I'll be gone most of the morning. Then I thought I might go play a round of golf," he says.

"It looks like it will be a perfect day for it," I reply.

"If you are back, you are welcome to join me," he says with a smile.

I look up at him. He is serious. I tell him I would like that very much, if the girls find dresses early in the day, then I will do that.

He smiles and plants a light kiss on my forehead and heads to the kitchen to grab some coffee.

It will really be nice to spend some time with him. Maybe we can talk about our relationship and I can tell him what I feel is missing without starting a fight. I'll finish my cup of tea and get the girls so we can get started shopping. I hope I'll be back in time to go to the golf course.

The girls take their time getting ready to leave but we are finally in my SUV by 930 am. They are both in good moods, excited to go shopping, and it is so nice to have them all to myself. I get sad thinking about how fast they have grown and how little time I have left with them at home. Everyone told me, once your children start school, the time flies by. Unfortunately, they were so right. It was just yesterday they started kindergarten. I miss those simple times. Now, they are so busy with school activities, homework, friends, and boys. I miss my little girls.

At the first shop, neither of them finds anything they liked. I agree, it seems like the dresses are more for bridal parties than school dances. At the second shop, Sarah finds the perfect dress as soon as she walks in the store. It is a beautiful fitted lavender gown, with spaghetti straps. The lavender color compliments her fair skin and light blue eyes. She looks so beautiful; I can't stop smiling at her. She is smiling too, so we know it is the one.

Two more shops, and Tabby found her dress. A short, royal blue dress with an open back. Both the color and cut of the dress are perfect for her and even though the back is open, it is age appropriate. She twirls around in front of the mirror.

"Do you think Daddy will like it, Mom?" she asks. She has always been daddy's little girl and always wants his approval.

"Yes, I think he will love it, baby," I tell her. "You look perfect."

"Ok, because if he doesn't like it, he won't let me go to the dance," she said.

"I know, but I have no doubts he will love it," I answer and smile proudly at her.

We go to another shop and find shoes, bracelets, and earrings that the girls think will be perfect with their new dresses. I suggest we get some lunch. They are famished and quickly agree.

I glance at my phone to check the time, it's 12:30 already and I notice I have a message from Andrew. I can't check it when I'm with the girls though, it will have to wait.

We go to one of our favorite Mexican restaurants. The food is great, as usual. The girls are busy chattering about the dance and what their friends are wearing. They aren't going together, but they are pairing up with other couples. My husband and I aren't yet comfortable with them dating alone, but we do allow them to go out in groups. They debate where the best places are to have a dinner before the dance and what their dates should wear. We all laugh that the boys probably haven't given it a passing thought yet.

We finish our meal and I pay the check. It's almost 1:30 in the afternoon now, so I tell the girls I am going to call home to let their dad know we are on our way. I try calling but there is no answer, so I try his cell phone. He answers on the fourth ring and there is quite a bit of noise in the background.

"Where are you?' he asks.

"We are getting on the road to come home. We just had lunch. Both the girls were able to find a dress, shoes and jewelry so today was a success. Where are you?" I ask him.

"I'm at the golf club, like I told you. Some of the guys are here so we are grabbing a drink and then heading out to play 18," he answers a little abruptly.

"Oh, okay. I'm sorry, I was looking forward to playing with you today," I say, hoping he will hear the disappointment in my voice.

"Grace, I knew you wouldn't be back in time when I asked you this morning. You always put the kids before me when I ask you to do something. Don't worry about it. I'm sure you had fun with them today. I'll just hang out with the guys here and play a round. I'll be home later. Gotta go, they are ready. I'll talk to you later."

I hear a click before I can say anything at all. So, his invitation wasn't an invitation at all? I feel bad, what does he mean, I put the kids first? It's not like they are small and need my constant attention. In fact, I feel like I don't see them much at all. Even less than I see him, really. They are all so busy. Even Seth, who doesn't have his driver's license yet, has a full schedule of his own activities and commitments.

I get in with the girls, who are still talking about the upcoming dance and other girl gossip. They are blasting the radio with music I don't even recognize. I look in the rear-view mirror as I back out of our parking space and see my reflection. I suddenly feel very old and alone. I look at the woman looking back at me. My eyes are bright and young but look very sad at this moment. I shake it off and just head home.

The girls' discussion is a nice distraction, but I am not really listening. Instead, I'm wondering what Andrew wrote to me. I hope he's still available to chat when I get home. It will be after midnight in Afghanistan but maybe he will still be up. I hope so. I suddenly miss him tremendously. I am so sorry I doubted him.

We get home and the girls head to their rooms, shutting their doors behind them. Seth is at a friend's house and won't be home until dinner. I get a cup of tea and settle with a blanket and my phone on the couch. I open the app we use. Last seen at....10:30 am. It's 3 pm here now and he is probably sleeping, but I write anyway.

"Baby, are you awake?" I hit send and set the phone in my lap. I click through some shows on tv, but nothing is holding my attention.

"Am here, honey. What are you doing? How was your day?" he responds.

I feel myself smile. "Were you sleeping Andrew? I'm sorry if I woke you. I was with my daughters all morning, getting their dresses for the spring formal and couldn't chat."

"Am awake. Don't be sorry, I'm always happy to hear from you. I know sometimes you are busy and can't talk. I understand. Did the girls find dresses?" he asks.

"Yes, both did, and they look so beautiful. How have you been? I'm so sorry about my email questioning everything you have told me. I feel terrible."

"Don't worry about that at all, Grace. You don't know what to expect with someone in my position. This is all new to you. I can literally be a ghost at a moment's notice, Grace. I can disappear if I need to, just like that. But I will never leave you, baby. Please don't worry about it anymore. Let's talk about other things. I am fine, the conference is over, finally. Now I can get back to my real job, you know how it is. I'm glad you had a nice day with the girls. You are such a wonderful mother, Grace. They are so blessed to have you. And I am so lucky to know you. I wish you were here in my bed with me. I would show you how much I love you and how much I treasure you."

His response makes me smile and feel that all is forgiven. "Thank you for understanding. I'm very sorry about all that again. This is all very new to me. I have never talked with anyone like this online, so my imagination runs wild sometimes. Andrew, I would love to be there with you, in your arms. But I would never want to let you out of my sight."

"Are you alone, Grace?"

"Yes, my husband and son are gone, and girls are in their rooms."

"Are you in your room?"

"No, I'm in the living room."

"Go to your room where you can have some privacy, baby. I want to call you."

My heart feels like it has stopped. I can't believe I'll actually hear his voice.

"Give me just a minute," I type back.

I try to catch my breath as I head to my bedroom. It's at the opposite end of the house as the children. I'm the last person the girls would be interested in, but I still listen down the hall for them before I go to my room and lock the door. I look in the mirror and straighten my hair and try to calm my nerves. I hate that my voice shakes when I am nervous, I hope he won't hear it.

"Ok, I'm alone now," I type.

It seems like I stare at my phone for an eternity. I put it down on my nightstand, I don't think it's cool to answer on the first ring, right? God, I am so nervous and have no idea what I'm doing.

Finally, it rings, he's calling me through the app since I have never given him my actual phone number. I take a few breaths, and answer.

The connection is not good at all and I am straining a bit to hear.

"Grace, how are you doing baby?" he says. I immediately notice he has an accent and doesn't sound American at all. Maybe a little Irish, I don't know because the connection is so bad.

"Hi, it's so good to hear your voice," I answer, but I'm getting a lot of echo when I talk. "Are you hearing an echo, Andrew?"

"No, I can hear you just fine, Grace. No issues at all," he says. I'm trying to figure out the accent, it almost has a middle east sound to it. I have a friend from New Delhi, and it's a bit like his, but not exactly.

"How are you, Grace? I'm so glad to talk to you finally," he says.

"I'm having a really hard time hearing you honey, I'm so sorry," I explain.

"It's okay, we can go back to our chat. I'll hang up now and write to you," he says. At least that's what I think he said, it sounds like we are underwater now. But now the line is dead, and he is gone.

"Are you there, baby? I love your voice, it's so calm and soft. It meant so much to me to hear your beautiful voice, Grace. I love it," his message appears, the phone is still in my hand.

I am so puzzled by his accent, but he was so sweet to call me. I really needed that today, especially after feeling like I was ditched by my husband.

"I'm sorry my connection was so bad, Andrew. I don't know what the problem was," I say.

"Don't worry, the calls through apps like this are VOIP and sometimes the quality isn't very good. We can try again some other time. Baby, it's almost 4am here, I have a flight training with the boys at 6am, I need to try to get some sleep, I'm sorry," he replied.

"I understand. I'm sorry for waking you. Please get some rest. Write me when you can. Be safe, Andrew," I write back.

"I will. Talk to you later, honey."

And with that, he is gone. I am still looking at the screen when his status changes from online to "Last seen at 3:30 pm". It always shows the time here. I wonder if I can set it to show me his time…probably not important, I'll just keep doing the math in my head. Kabul is 11 hours, 30 minutes ahead on my time here. I was curious and googled why it is 30 minutes off from most other time zones. The best answer I found was because they can. So, there you go. Who am I to argue with that?

CHAPTER 16

My husband returned home after dark. I had made dinner at our normal time so by now everyone had eaten and had gone to their rooms for the evening. I was sitting at the kitchen table grading some essays and drinking a cup of tea.

"Have you eaten? How did you play?" I look up from my laptop and smile at him.

"Yes, we ate in the clubhouse, I figured you and the kids went ahead without me. I played okay. I really need to make a point to get out there more and work on my short game," he said.

"How were the guys? Can I fix you a drink?" I ask.

"Just some ice water, please, that's all. It was the usual, the guys complain about their jobs and say their kids are ungrateful considering how hard they work for everything they've given to them. They were talking about getting all of together to go on a golf trip," he says and quickly adds, "Just the guys, no wives or kids."

"Oh, when would they want to do that? Can you take the time away with all the projects you have going right now?" I ask, handing him a glass of ice water and thinking, here we go, this is how separate vacations get started.

"Probably in a month. Dave is going to get his travel agent on it. We will probably go to Augusta, depending on the cost. You know how cheap some of those guys can be," he answered.

"Wow, that sounds nice. I guess your guys can handle things while you are gone," I say.

"Yes, I don't have any doubts there. They can always call me if something comes up. But we will have at least two projects done by then, and we only have one on the horizon, but it will have started at that time. So, all the bugs should be worked out by then. Grace, were you upset that I didn't wait for you today?" he asked.

I take a long sip of my tea before responding. Here's my chance.

"To be honest, yes. I feel like we are living separate lives. And not just recently, it has been this way for a while. I don't know what to think. I love you very much, but you just don't seem very interested in me anymore." I say. I feel myself shaking a bit and feel cold. I take another sip of tea, hoping that the warmth will settle my nerves.

"I could say the same. You are always busy with your job, teaching, and the kids. You always have to have the house a certain way. I know you are dealing with your parents and your mom's health too. We just seem to have different interests now," he says.

"I'm confused. You work night and day, but you are saying how busy *I* am with *my* job? I guarantee you put in more hours than I do. And I often work at home, because you and the kids are busy with your own things, so I need to keep busy," I say, noticing my voice starting to shake. I get up to take my cup to the kitchen. "And about the house, you have always said your home reflects your work and your business. You need to have everything perfect because that's what your clients like to see. I would be happy with a modest home, but this was a priority for you."

"Grace, I have to do my paperwork at home, I don't always have office time during the day," he says.

"What about the secretary you hired to help with the paperwork and billing last year? It doesn't seem like she has taken anything off your plate." I pause and noticed that he is looking out the window. I suddenly feel like someone punched me in the stomach. Oh my god, I can't believe I am so stupid. Of course, this all makes sense now, she is in her late twenties, long brown hair....

"What is it, Grace? Stop. Really? I know that jealous look. You are completely wrong. She is engaged. There is nothing between us except I'm her boss. That's it. So, get that out of your head," his voice raises a bit, but I can tell he knows that I know. I can't prove it, but I know.

"Ok, sure, I understand. I don't mean anything against her," I say, walking to the sink with my empty cup.

"You have nothing to worry about, Grace. You have me for the long haul. I'm going to shower and go to bed; it's been a long day," he says as he is walking away toward the bedroom.

I know I'm right; I could see it in his eyes. Maybe he hasn't acted on it, but it's there. He said I have nothing to worry about, I have him for the long haul. Have what for the long haul? This life? It is worth it? I'm comfortable, I have all my needs met and the children will go to college and have a great start. But I'm supposed to sit back and let this happen behind my back? I remember his friend, Kyle, cheated on his wife a few years ago. It was a nasty divorce; I would never want my family to go through that. I shudder remembering how horrible it was to watch.

I walk back the table and close out of the university learning system software. I can't focus enough to provide decent feedback tonight. I log off and stare at a blank screen. Of course, I'm no better than he is. I suddenly feel very guilty for talking to Andrew. Since our first chat on Christmas, I have given my heart to him; someone I've never even met in person. How pathetic is that? My marriage was on rocky ground and I didn't even acknowledge it. It didn't take much to make me have feelings for him since my needs aren't being fulfilled here at home. Should I feel bad? Yes, probably. My husband would be furious if he knew. But at least, unlike him, I'm not in the same office very day, flirting or God knows what. I feel the tears starting to come. I just want to be desired and to be happy. Andrew makes me feel both. I wrap up with my favorite blanket and curl up on the couch, trying to be quiet because I really don't want to talk to anyone right now. I hope my husband will just go to sleep after his shower and not look for me. I try to sink deeper into the couch, tears still running down my face. Finally sleep comes to me.

CHAPTER 17

At 3am, I can hear my husband talking. What is he saying? Who is calling at this hour? I hear him say, okay, I'll let her know, we will head that way. What is going on? God, my head hurts. I remember now, I cried myself to sleep, that explains my throbbing headache.

"Grace, are you awake? You need to get up. That was your dad. He is taking your mother to the hospital and wants you to come," my husband explains and now I'm fully awake.

"Oh my God, what is going on? What happened to her? I thought she was responding well to the chemo. What did he say?" I am rubbing my eyes, trying to get untangled from the blanket and get my feet on the floor.

"He said she has had a setback. She was having trouble breathing so he called an ambulance. He is following them to the ER," he explains, sitting down next to me on the couch. "You need to get in the shower so you can go, your dad sounds like he really needs you. Your sister is flying in from New York as soon as she can get things arranged. I'll get your suitcase started for you."

"Are you not going with me?" I ask, incredulous. I swear I heard him say we will head that way, not Grace will head that way.

"No, hon. There isn't anything the kids or I can do at this point. Your dad just asked for you to come. We would be in the way. They have school and I would be tied to my phone and laptop the whole time anyway. We can come if you think we need to once you get there and assess the situation. He may just be taking extra precautions; you know how protective he is of your mom," he says.

"I would hope he is protective; she is his wife; she took care of him for fifty years. It's the least he can do. Fine, if you can't go, I get it," I snap at him and rush to the shower.

In the shower, I make a mental list of the people I need to call to tell them I will be unavailable for a few days. Of course, I will wait until a decent hour to call. I realize it's only 330 am. After my shower, I finish the packing my husband started and grab the mug of hot tea he prepared. I check my purse and decide to run by the ATM before the four-hour drive ahead of me.

"Call me when you get there, okay? Be safe. I'm sure everything will be fine, Grace, don't worry," my husband leans in for a kiss goodbye and I unconsciously turn my head, so he only gets my cheek.

"Yeah, I'll keep you posted," I say as I get in my car in the dark garage. I connect my phone to Bluetooth and back out. The early morning is quiet, and the streets are empty, it's too early for any commuters and the neighbors who get out to walk each morning. After I go through the ATM, I call my sister. I know she will be awake, it's an hour ahead in New York and apparently it sounds like dad called her first.

"Hello, hey sis. Are you already on the road?" Claire answers on the second ring, the noise in the background sounds like she is on the train heading into the city.

"Yes, just left. I should get there at about 8 or so. Are you on your way?" I respond.

"Not quite. I'm running into the office and then will get to the airport. I have to drop off some files for a court case tomorrow," she says. Claire is a paralegal for a very big law firm in New York. She has a longtime boyfriend, Scott, but they never married, lived together, or had children. He works for an investment firm and is a terrific guy. I sometimes envy what I perceive as her freedom. She never acts as if she would like her life any different. She's content and so much fun. My kids think she is the greatest person ever. She is a great listener to all their stories, and they fight for her attention when she visits. I am so glad she is coming to the hospital today.

"What time does your flight leave?" I ask.

"It is scheduled for 11am but there is fog this morning, but hopefully it will clear out by then. I'll get a rental car and head straight to the hospital so I should see you at about 3 or 4 this afternoon," she answers.

"So, Claire, what do you think about this setback, as dad called it? It took me by surprise. We were there a few weeks ago and she seemed to be doing well. Just tired, but that's to be expected," I tell her.

"I don't know. Dad called last week and said her oncologist wasn't very optimistic at the last appointment that she was responding well to the chemo. At first, she was, but now she isn't. He said sometimes that happens, so they may have to consider other options," she explained with the noise of the train in the background.

"Oh, I haven't talked to him this week. I had a full schedule and didn't call, I wish I had now," I say. My stomach feels like it's in knots. How could I be so self-involved? I count the days; a whole week has passed, and I haven't checked on them.

"I'm sure she will be fine, Grace. Dad is very cautious with her, he always was, but especially now. We will just have to hear what the doctors say when we get there. I'm almost to my stop, Grace. I'll talk to you soon, drive safe, okay?" And with that, Claire is gone.

I am now past the downtown area and have about three and a half hours to drive. It's still a bit too early to call my boss and my secretary, Sophia. I've avoided the morning rush hour traffic though. My mind wanders to Andrew. Since I'm driving, I decide to send a voice note to him on the app.

"Hi Andrew. I would say good morning but it's not. My dad called at 3 am and said mom is having trouble breathing. He called an ambulance. My sister is flying in from New York and I'm driving there to be with them. I don't know what I'll find when I get there. I just found out from my sister that even though things were going well when I last saw her, at the last appointment, the oncologist said mom isn't responding to the chemo. I feel so bad, Andrew, I am the worst daughter. I have been so busy this last week I haven't called them at all. I had no idea that they got this bad news.

I hope you are safe and doing well. I just wish I could talk to you. I have some other things to tell you as well, but I can't right now. I'm sorry for this terrible message, I hope you can understand me, I just can't stop crying. I'm going to find a place to stop. I need to get something hot to drink and settle my emotions before I call my boss. Write me if you can, I don't know if I will be able to write you back, but I just wanted you to know why if you don't hear from me. I love you, Andrew. Thank you for everything you are to me. I don't know what I would do without you right now. Take care, honey."

I stop at a gas station at the next exit and hit send without playing it back. I may have sounded like a mess and I hope he can understand it, but that's me right now. He said he loves everything about me. Well, Andrew, here's me falling apart.

I check my face in the visor mirror and apply some makeup before going into the store. After getting back to the SUV and taking a few sips of some very strong coffee, I call my boss. He tells me to take all the time I need; he will get another manager to cover what can't wait. I thank him and tell him I will keep him informed once I know more. I call Sophia and ask her to clear my calendar for this week. She is wonderful and I know she will take care of everything in my absence. It's so nice to have one less thing to worry about right now.

I ease back onto the interstate and start to feel a little better. The commuter traffic is starting to pick up a little and I can just see the sun on the horizon. My phone rings and I hit the Bluetooth button. It's my children calling to check on me and ask questions about their grandma. I tell them not to worry, and that I will call as soon as I know something. I assure them that they should go to school and their activities. Both the girls are talking at the same time and tell me they love me and to be careful. My son finally gets the phone away from his sisters.

"Mom, is grandma going to be okay?" I can hear the worry in his voice. He and I are a lot alike. He loves with his entire heart and can spot someone hurting or in need of a friend a mile away.

"I think so, baby. They will check her out at the hospital to be sure. She gets weak easily during her treatment, so they will do what is needed to get her strength back," I answer.

"When will you be home?" he asks.

"Probably in a couple of days, baby. Will you call me when you get home from school this afternoon? I would really love to talk to you," I answer.

"Sure, Mom, I will. Just drive safe, okay? I need to go; the girls are in the car waiting for me," he says.

We both say I love you once more and hang up. I just realize I haven't heard from my husband this morning. As I think about our conversation last night and decide to wait until he calls me. I really don't need any additional stress this morning.

CHAPTER 18

I arrive at the hospital at 8:30 am and head straight to the ER reception desk. I did some of my pharmacy residency at this hospital, so I know where to go. At the reception desk, after looking at a computer screen, they tell me mom has been admitted and give me the room number. I get a sinking feeling about that; I was hopeful this was a false alarm and she would have been sent home.

I see dad in one of the waiting rooms as I get off the elevator. He looks very alone and scared sitting there. I practically run to him.

"Dad, I'm here! How are you? How's mom? What's going on?" I throw my purse down in the chair next him and he stands to give me a hug.

"I'm so glad you are here, Grace. I don't think I can sit here another second longer," he says, and from the look on his face, he isn't exaggerating.

"Can we see her? What are they saying?" I feel like I'm pummeling him with questions, and he hasn't really answered one of them yet.

"Not right now, they are getting her ready for a test. They think she may have a pulmonary embolism, which would explain why she was so short of breath," he explains. "Let's go get some coffee, there's nothing we can do right now."

"Ok, sure. Have you eaten anything this morning? Let's get some breakfast too." I hold his arm as we start toward the elevator. Sometimes his blood sugar gets a little low and I would bet money he hasn't eaten a bite this morning. We both need each other to be strong right now so we should eat while we can.

We grab some food and find a table by a window that overlooks a garden area. I remember from my residency that this hospital does have a pretty good cafeteria and they don't disappoint today either. We both eat a few bites before talking.

"I spoke with Claire when she was on the train this morning. I am glad she is coming too," I smile at Dad. I know he is glad to have his girls at home, despite the circumstances.

"Yes, I called her first since she gets up so early and is an hour ahead of us. I didn't want to wake your whole family, especially on a school night. But I had to let you know," he says, eating slowly.

"Oh Dad, you didn't wake up the kids. They are teenagers, remember? You would have performed a miracle waking them up early. I talked with them this morning before school. They are worried about grandma, but I told them we really wouldn't know anything until later today anyway. School will keep their minds occupied so hopefully they won't worry too much," I tell him.

"You have wonderful children, Grace. And you are a wonderful mom, don't ever forget that. It can be tough raising teenagers sometimes, but you have a good bunch," he says with a smile. Agreeing, I smile back at him.

We sit, glancing out the window, eating our breakfast, and trying to not worry. We are doing pretty good being strong for one another, all things considered. My phone buzzes in my bag. I glance at it in my purse.

"If you need to take it, go ahead Grace, I'm not going anywhere," Dad smiles at me. "I know you and Claire moved heaven and earth to clear schedules to be here today. I appreciate it too. Go ahead, check your messages. I'm going to get some more coffee and eggs."

I step outside. The weather is beautiful today, Mom would love to be outside working with her flowers on a day like this. I pull my phone from my purse and read the message from Andrew.

"Grace, I'm so sorry about your mom. Call me on the app as soon as you can. Not while you are driving though. Love, Andrew."

I connect to the hospital Wi-Fi so I can call through the app. Maybe that will help me get a better connection. Funny, I still remember the Wi-Fi password from my time here.

He answers on the second ring. My heart is beating so fast, but I am so glad to be able to talk to him.

"Grace," he greets me in his deep voice, "can you hear me baby? You aren't driving, are you?"

"Andrew, yes, I'm here and the connection is much better. No, I'm not driving. I'm at the hospital. Mom has been admitted, they think she has a blood clot in her lung, which explains why it's hard for her to breathe. She also isn't responding to the chemotherapy now. So, we will see what the doctors suggest about starting other chemo drugs." I notice the slight accent again, but I am so relieved to talk to him, that I am not going to let my mind question it.

"You are at the hospital now? Where is your family?" he asks with genuine concern in your voice.

"I'm here with dad. He's getting more coffee right now. My sister is flying in and should be here this afternoon," I answer.

"Your family isn't there?" he asks.

"No, the children went to school; there isn't much for them to do until we know more anyway. My husband is at work, I guess. I haven't talked to him since I left this morning. He said he had some projects at work that he couldn't leave," I say.

"What? He isn't there with you? What the hell? He let you drive four hours away when you are sick with worry about your mother? What kind of man does that? I swear, Grace, I would never leave you to deal with this alone. Promise me this right now. You will call me anytime, day or night. I am here, whatever you need. If I can't send you what you need, I will make a phone call, and you'll have it. I swear to God. I am just thankful you didn't have a car accident this morning. You were crying on your message, Grace. It broke my heart. But now, it makes me furious to know you were all alone," he tells me. His voice is so powerful, so commanding. I feel like I just got a glimpse into what his boys hear every day.

"It's okay, Andrew. I'm okay now. I don't need anything. I'm just waiting, there's nothing anyone can do. My husband felt like he should give Dad, Claire, and me some time together with Mom. He said he will come if I need him," I feel ridiculous making excuses, even when I know Andrew is right. He should be here with me. But instead, he is at work, with his gorgeous secretary. I can't let my mind do this to me; not now.

"Ok, if you say so. I would not have let you go on your own though. That is pathetic. But I'll trust you and not say another word about it," his voice is softer now. "Tell me about your mom's health, Grace. Will they be able to help her? Part of my job is visiting the sick and injured here on base. I hate going, I never know what to say, I always feel like I'm in the way. I so admire people like you in healthcare. You all have a special gift."

"Well, thank you, but sometimes we don't know what to say either. Just being there or holding someone's hand can mean everything. Right now, mom is getting a scan to determine if it is a pulmonary embolism. If it is, then she will be given medication to thin her blood and break up the clot, and hopefully, prevent any more from forming. About the chemotherapy, she will have a series of scans to see if the tumor has shrunk, grown, spread, or stayed the same. Since she is on treatment, we expect it to have shrunk, but not all tumors and/or patients respond well. They will likely change her chemotherapy drug or regimen. Worst case would be that it has spread, but right now, they must treat the embolism. Most likely, they will evaluate the tumor response when she is discharged. The embolism could kill her," I say.

"Ok, thank you for telling me. I will remember her in my prayers. Now, I just want to know that you are okay. Where will you stay tonight?" he asks me.

"I think Claire and I will stay at our parents. They still live in the house in which we grew up. Mom never really changed our rooms much after we moved out. So, imagine that, I'll sleep in the same bed I did as a teenager," I attempt a laugh. It is funny to think after all these years, my room looks the same, just cleaner than I kept it.

"I know you are a comfort to your dad. I'll let you go, Grace. You need to be with him. Please write me later when you can or if anything changes." His voice is so kind as we say goodbye. The last thing I hear is, "I love you so much, Grace. Whatever you need, just say the word and it's yours."

Back in the cafeteria, dad is reading the paper and sipping his coffee. I notice his empty plate of eggs and remains of a cinnamon roll. He must have been famished. He looks up at me and smiles.

"Grace let's go upstairs and see what the nurses know. Then, if we still can't see your mom, we will go home for a little bit. I just threw these clothes on this morning. I'd really like a shower and to shave," Dad says. I hadn't noticed earlier but he does look a bit unshaven. He has always taken pride in his appearance. Even mowing the lawn or working in his garage, he looks groomed and tidy. Much credit goes to Mom too. She taught me how to iron a man's shirt when I was in grade school. I wasn't too happy about my lessons at the time nor was I happy when she made me do it over until it was perfect. But as an adult, I find a peace-fulness working in my laundry room and making perfect creases.

The nurses didn't have any update and said mom will be probably be about an hour longer in the Nuclear Medicine department getting her scan. We head to the parking lot and drive separately to my parents' home.

CHAPTER 19

Pulling into their drive behind Dad, I smile at their perfectly manicured lawn. The whole world could be in shambles, and this wouldn't change. It brings me such comfort. Entering through the side door, the smell of home enters my lungs. I love it here. I need this. Dad turns and says, "You know where everything is, make yourself at home. Your mom keeps the bathroom and kitchen stocked just like you and Claire still live here, so take whatever you need."

"Thanks Dad. I appreciate it," I say, smiling at him.

I place my suitcase on the cedar chest at the foot of my bed. Now it's full of extra quilts, but when I was a teenager, it held yearbooks, keepsakes, and my teddy bear I thought I was too old for, but always was there when I needed him. After my shower, I practically collapse onto the bed for a much-needed nap.

About an hour later, I slowly wake and smile when I see my room. It's just like it was years ago. I can hear Dad on the phone down the hall. It sounds like he is talking to the hospital. I brush my hair and put a little makeup on. I want to give him some privacy, I'm not sure if he is talking to Mom or the doctor.

When I hear him say goodbye, I straighten the bed and then walk out to see if he has any news.

"Hey, sleepyhead," he says with a smile.

"Hi Dad, sorry, I didn't realize how tired I was," I say, "Was that the hospital?"

"Yes, and right before that, Claire called to say she landed safely and should be here in about an hour. She is going to come here so we can all ride together," Dad explains.

"Good idea. Did the doctor have any results or updates?" I ask, realizing I am bracing myself for bad news.

"I talked to the oncologist. She said that it is a pulmonary embolism that is causing her to be short of breath. They placed her on oxygen to help her breathing and a blood thinner to try to break up that clot and prevent any more. She will be in the hospital for a few days at least. They are going to use the time to do some other tests while she is there, to see if the tumor was responding to treatment," he says.

"Ok, that's good. How is Mom feeling? Did you get to talk to her?" I ask.

"No, she was sleeping, but I told the doctor we will be there shortly to see her. You girls may have questions for the nurses I wouldn't think to ask," he says.

"Okay, are you hungry, Dad? Let me make you something to eat while we are waiting for Claire," I offer.

"Sure, sounds good. Whatever you see in the kitchen, is fair game. I'm really glad you are here, Grace," he says and smiles at me.

"Me too, Dad. Kick back in your recliner and I'll bring your plate to you."

We are almost finished eating the sandwiches I made when Claire arrives with enough luggage for a year. She sees the look on my face and laughs.

"Grace, you know me. I come prepared for any potential wardrobe situation. I brought some work with me too," Claire says.

"You must have everything including Halloween costumes with you. Good grief, Claire, it's called packing wardrobe essentials not your own Nordstrom store," I laugh, helping her lug everything to her child-hood bedroom.

"Just like I remember, God bless our mother, Grace. She knows how to maintain a time capsule," Claire says.

"Do you need something to eat? Or anything before we go to the hospital?" I ask.

"Stop, Grace, I know you won't know what to do with yourself if you don't have anyone to take care of, but I can fend for myself," Claire laughs, "I'm just going to brew a strong cup of coffee and then we can go."

While the coffee is brewing, the three of us chat, about Claire's flight, Dad's landscaping, my children, and our jobs. I don't think any of us are ready to talk about Mom's health yet.

We all take a cup of coffee to go and Dad drives us to the hospital.

"Yuck, I hate this place," Claire says. "I can't even drive by here without thinking of Granddad in ICU and Grandma's last days."

Since I'm in the medical field, I forget that for many people, hospitals bring back terrible memories. I get to see all sides of it, the newborn who is just as perfect as her parents prayed she would be, the patient that is cured of cancer, the young athlete who finishes physical therapy stronger than before, as well as the unhappy stories. For Claire, it's been mostly unhappy. She will shut down if anyone brings her up, but I know she is thinking of her seventeen-year-old self in the ER, screaming because her best friend was killed by a drunk driver. I reach forward from the back seat and squeeze her shoulder. She holds my hand for a minute until Dad pulls the car into a spot as close as we can get to the front door.

Mom is in a good mood when we arrive, smiling at us as we enter. The nurse gives us all the same update that Dad heard earlier from the oncologist and says we can stay for no more than 30 minutes then Mom needs her rest. We agree to the rules as we all take turns hugging and kissing Mom. She is a bit pale and looks even smaller with the oxygen mask taking up most of her pretty face. Dad sits in the chair by her bed and pats her arm frequently. The IV drip is giving her the heparin she needs to dissolve the clot. We are all telling stories, laughing and really enjoying our visit. The 30 minutes is gone before we know it and the nurse peeks in the room, asking Mom how she is feeling. I know this is our clue to leave. Claire and I kiss Mom and tell her we will be back in the morning, leaving Dad to have a few moments alone with her.

CHAPTER 20

In the waiting room, Claire looks me up and down.

"You look different, Grace. What's been going on?" she asks.

"What do you mean different? I don't think I look any different, I'm still the same as I always was," I am a bad liar and Claire knows it.

"Ok, but I brought a bottle of red wine that will tell me the truth later," she has an infectious laugh and is better than the CIA at getting people to talk, alcohol or not.

Later that night, after we got takeout for dinner and Dad had gone to bed, I'm in my old room, checking my messages. Each of the kids have tried to call and I have a couple of messages on the app from Andrew. No messages from my husband though. I call home.

"Mom, mom, mom, what's going on with Grandma?" all three kids are fighting for the phone.

"Slow down, babies, one at a time. Grandma is doing ok; she has a blood clot in her lung, but they are giving her medicine. She will have to be in the hospital for a few days, but I got to visit with her tonight and she sends her love to you all," I tell them to take turns and I'll talk to each of them.

Tabby gets the phone first and tells me everything that happened at school, what homework she has and all the important stuff in her teenage life. She tells me she loves me and then lets my son have the phone.

"Mom, are you doing ok? How's Grandad?" he asks. He is so sweet, always thinking of everyone else before sharing the details of his day. I tell him Grandad is looking forward to taking him golfing when he gets out of school and that he is going to show him that top secret fishing hole now that he is old enough to keep his mouth shut and not tell anyone where the big ones are. My son laughs at that. He and Dad are so much alike. They act like best buds whenever they are together.

When Sarah has her turn, I ask her if her dad is there. She says no, he ordered a couple of pizzas for their dinner, but he was working late. That explains why he hasn't messaged me at all today. I have a sinking suspicion that he isn't alone at the office. We talk a bit longer and I tell each one I love them before we hang up.

I am so furious at my husband. He can't even spare a couple of seconds to send a text to make sure I'm okay. This makes me almost certain my feelings are right. I head to my sister's room across the hall; that glass of red wine sounds perfect right now.

She is on the phone with Scott but tells him she needs to go when she sees my face. They hang up after a sweet 'I love you, I love you' more exchange.

"I believe you said something about wine?" I ask, giving her the best pitiful, my life sucks face I can.

"Oh lord, yes, I can see this isn't a time for moderation! Wait, let me get some glasses and then you can talk. What is going on?" She runs to the kitchen and back in just seconds with two large wine glasses.

I tell her everything about my marriage. The sleeping arrangements, the un-vitiation for a round of golf, the no wives trip that is being planned and my suspicion about the secretary. When I am done, my glass is empty and I feel better, but Claire looks furious.

"Ok, I'm trying to not jump to conclusions, but the evidence is certainly saying he is guilty. Or at least wants to be guilty," Claire's forehead is crinkled in thought. "And he told you not to be ridiculous when it got awkward when his secretary was brought up?"

"Yes, I didn't accuse him of anything. I just said I thought he'd hired a secretary to take some things off his plate, but it seems like he is bringing even more work home now," I say.

"Well, it could be that she is completely incompetent, and he doesn't have the guts to fire her," Claire offers. "But I don't think so, Grace. I would be very cautious. Do you still have your mad money account? A girl should always be prepared for anything," Claire attempts a smile. A mad money account is something Mom told us to start when we were just teenagers and keep secret from everyone else, especially husbands. One of her older sisters married a guy with a bad gambling problem and her mad money was her salvation when she finally left him.

"I do. In fact, all these years I have continued to put a little bit aside every month. I have close to fifty thousand now," I tell her.

"That's my sister, always doing the responsible thing," Claire teased. "But seriously, you may need it someday. Hopefully, you are wrong, but it can't hurt to be prepared."

I see Claire glance at the time on her phone. I took a nap this afternoon, but she must be exhausted.

"Love you, sis. I am so glad you are here. I'm going to let you get some rest," I say.

"Yeah, I better go to sleep. It's been a long day. I love you too Grace. Good night."

I cross the hall and hop into the bed I slept in for so many years. Happy years, but there were some tears and sleepless nights too. Speaking of which, I still haven't heard from my husband.

I send him a brief text, just telling him about mom. A few minutes later he responds, apologizing for not calling and glad to hear that she is stable. He tells me good night and to call if anything changes. Honestly, I think I would have gotten more emotion from the guy at the gas station.

CHAPTER 21

I have a few messages in the chat from Andrew asking for any update and if I have eaten or had any rest. He is so thoughtful. I write back, not expecting him to come online.

"Grace? How are you? Tell me everything baby, I am so glad to hear from you. Can I call you? I am dying to hear your voice."

"Yes, please do. I think my dad and sister are both asleep and I am in my own room, so it won't wake them," I type.

His call comes quickly, and I am smiling as I answer.

"Andrew? Hi, thank you so much for being so thoughtful. You have no idea what a comfort you have been today," I say.

"Don't say thank you. If only I could be there! I would do anything to help you and your family get through this. I don't want you to worry about anything. I will get you whatever you need," he says. "Have you slept? Have you eaten?"

"Yes, I took a nap earlier. I don't have much of an appetite, but I did eat, and I feel fine. We will go to see Mom in the morning as soon as they allow her to have visitors. I hope we are there when the doctor makes rounds after she has the test to determine if her tumor is responding. I am curious to know if they will change her chemotherapy medication," I explain. "How was your day? Were you busy?"

"I had some office time and caught up on paperwork, nothing exciting. Tomorrow we will be doing some training, so I won't be able to write to you until later."

"Oh, okay, I'll send you an update if I have one and you just write when you are free."

"Grace are you in bed?" he asks.

"Yes, I'm lying in bed," I reply. "It must be morning there?"

"It's almost 10 am but I am still in my room. Are you tired or would you like to talk?" His voice is lower, softer, and kind.

"I'm not tired. I really enjoying talking to you," I say.

"Good, honey. I will never tire of talking to you. You are such a beautiful woman. You should be appreciated and loved by everyone around you. But no one can love you more than I do. These feelings I have are overwhelming. Every day, I think about what our lives will be like once we are together. Every single day, Grace, brings us closer to that day. Tell me, what are you wearing as you lay in bed tonight, Grace?" he asks.

I feel myself blush. "I have a black tank top and panties on, that's it."

"Beautiful......I am imagining the contrast of the black against your fair skin. I want to be beside you. I want you to relax with me. I want to help you forget about the world tonight. Would you like that, my queen?"

"Yes," I say softly. "Very, very much."

"Let me tell you every touch you will feel. Every place on your beautiful body I will caress and kiss...Everything we will experience together. I will make love to you like you deserve, like you desire. Be with me now Grace. Close your beautiful eyes. It's only the two of us in this room.... I love you so much baby.... Listen to me my love. I am going to tell you everything I will do......"

And he did. All the way from the other side of the globe, it was the most wonderful thing I have ever experienced.

CHAPTER 22

My alarm went off at 5 am, just like every morning. I felt wonderful, thank you, Andrew my love. The world is beautiful, and I am so happy. I decided to go for a short run. Dad and Claire were still asleep when I returned, so I started some coffee for them and the tea kettle for me. I took a hot shower, then called home to be sure the kids were up for school. They were awake but moving slow. I talked with each of them and wished them a good day at school. They promised to call me as soon as they arrive home. Interesting, none of them mentioned their dad and I have no messages from him this morning.

I think I'll just do a little check in on him. His phone rings a few times before he answers.

"Hello, Grace? What's wrong?" He sounds like he was sleeping.

"Nothing. I just thought I would say good morning and check on things," I say.

"Oh, okay. Sorry, I was still sleeping" he answers.

"Where are you? I've already talked to the kids this morning" I emphasize this so he can't lie and say he is at home.

"Oh, I fell asleep at the office. I was drawing up some plan options for that commercial project I told you about and it was after midnight when I finished. So, I just slept here in my office. This couch is very uncomfortable, by the way," he says.

"Ok, well I better go. I hear Dad and Claire. We are all anxious to get to the hospital."

"Ok, is your Mom doing better? Tell her I'm thinking of her," he says.

"Last night she was in good spirits. They are giving her a blood thinner and she had a good appetite for dinner, so that's promising," I say.

"Ok, well, be careful. Call me tonight," he says, sounding anxious to get off the phone.

"Yes, I will. Talk to you then." That's when I hear her. She drops something in the background, and I hear her voice. He's not alone. And I know exactly who he is with. I am suddenly sick to my stomach. I drop my phone and run to the bathroom, barely making it there before throwing up. I am so sick, the room is spinning, I have to lay down or I will pass out. I try to put my head between my knees to get some blood to my head, but I end up on the cold tile floor. The cold is a welcome relief to the burning in my cheeks. The tunnel vision is closing in and I close my eyes as the world goes black.

CHAPTER 23

"Grace? Grace! Wake up honey. Wake up. Don't move. Here, slow down. Don't move too fast. Are you alright? What happened?" Claire is wiping my face with a towel and looking very concerned. I must look like hell.

"Oh God, Claire. I'm so sorry. I am so upset. Don't tell Dad I did this, okay? Where is he? Does he know I did this? I don't want him to worry," I plead, tears are streaming down my face.

"No, no, honey, he is outside talking to the neighbors. They are all asking about Mom and some brought food over for him. I just came into your room looking for you," she says, still very concerned. "Are you sick? What happened?"

"He's cheating on me, Claire. I heard her, his secretary when I was on the phone with him. He didn't go home last night. Said he was working late and slept at his office on the couch," I say, hoping she can understand me through my tears.

"Oh my god, sis, I'm so sorry. Come here, it's going to be okay. I'll get you through this, whatever it takes," she says, holding me, trying to get me to stop shaking. "Here, let's get you wrapped up, you are freezing, and this floor is not comfortable."

She helps me to the bed and locks the door, so Dad doesn't come in and see me. Claire crawls up beside me and holds me in her arms like a baby. I can't stop shaking.

"Thank you, Claire. Thank God you are here. What am I going to do? Should I go home? He left the kids by themselves last night. I know they are teenagers, but they had no idea he was even gone all night, just that he was going to work late. Should I confront him? What do I tell the kids?" My mind is racing, panicked.

"You are going to do nothing. Not one thing. You are going to lay here. I'll get you some toast and hot tea. Then we will see how you feel. You are not going home. The kids are fine. I talked to them last night before you did, and they were watching a movie and eating pizza. They are okay now and they will be okay no matter what. Don't worry about them. Do you think the jerk knows you heard her?"

"I think so, he has to know I heard that noise and then her saying something. She was probably apologizing for making noise and ruining his lie," I say. I am starting to get calmed down a little and the room isn't spinning anymore.

"Don't try to stand up. In fact, don't move at all. Be right back, I'll get you that tea and toast," Claire says as she goes down the hall.

I hear her open the front door and say hi to the neighbors. I close my eyes and hear her tell dad that I had to make some calls to work and will be a little while. I feel like crying again but I won't let myself. I'm starting to get really pissed. He isn't worth it. He's been distant from me from for a while. I probably shouldn't be surprised. What man doesn't want to make love to his wife? Or sleep next to her? Here I am without my husband while my mother is lying in a hospital bed and he is with his girlfriend. Or whatever she is. It doesn't matter what she is to him. He's a piece of shit to me.

Claire returns with the toast and some steaming tea. I slowly move into a sitting position to take a sip. Suddenly, I'm very hungry and eat both pieces of toast while Claire and I discuss my newfound situation.

"My advice is to take your time with this, Grace. Do you want a divorce? I've seen way too many women rush to get a divorce because they are so angry. When your emotions are high, you lose the ability to be calculating and shrewd. You are smart and you must watch out for your interests. You put a lot and energy and time into your marriage. You are wise to take your time," Claire says. Of course, as a paralegal she has seen it all.

"I honestly don't know what I want. Of course, I love him, we built our lives together. I hate that we have drifted apart so far that it's come to this. I should have tried harder for his attention, worked harder at communication, I guess. But when he constantly ignores me or just says he's too busy over and over, I get tired of asking. I have felt distant from him too. When you don't have a physical relationship, the emotions fade away."

I am not going to tell her about Andrew. I feel hypocritical blaming my husband for everything when I'm in love with someone else. It's best if I just keep that a secret.

"I understand. It's best to take some time to think it all through. It's probably good that you aren't at home right now. How are you feeling? Do you feel like going to the hospital?" Claire asks.

"Yes, I want to see Mom. Don't say anything to either of them though, please. I don't want them to worry about any of this," I ask her.

"You bet. I'll go see what Dad is doing. You get ready to go. Love you sis. You and the kids are going to be okay. Don't worry about anything," Claire says, giving me a peck on my forehead as she leaves.

I walk into the bathroom to get ready. I honestly feel better. Claire is right. I will be okay. I think in the depths of my heart I knew my marriage was in shambles. Oddly, I feel a sense of relief. Hearing her on the phone was horrible, but it confirmed what I saw in his eyes when I mentioned her. The kids, though, how will they handle this? I feel myself start to tear up again. I can't get emotional right now. I need to be strong and visit my mother. My parents need me. I'll focus on them and not think about this anymore. I can't do anything about it anyway.

CHAPTER 24

We get to the hospital just as Mom is getting her lunch. Her nurse today is Mary, someone I knew from my residency days. We catch up on the hospital gossip for a little bit, while Dad has some private time with Mom and Claire calls her office. She says Mom is in good spirits and her labs were good this morning. The doctors made rounds early and were pleased with her progress. She tells Claire and I to go on in, she'll overlook the two visitors only rule for us. I get a quick hug and thank her for everything she has been doing for Mom.

Mom looks wonderful today. She is smiling and laughing with us. The first thing she asks is for her mirror and a hairbrush, so we help her find both so she will feel more like herself. She didn't eat much, but I have never known her to have a big appetite. We have a wonderful morning visiting and reminiscing. She and Dad are holding hands as we talk. Claire and I exchange glances occasionally, they are so sweet with one another.

We get to stay in her room for almost 3 hours before we are asked to step out. Some lab tests have been ordered and an EKG so she will be busy for a while. We give Mom hugs and decide to head to the cafeteria to get a bite to eat.

"I'm famished. Too bad we didn't bring some of the food the neighbors brought over. It all really looked great," Dad said.

"It really did. That was so nice of your neighbors to do that, Dad," Claire says.

"Your mom is always the first one with a casserole or dessert whenever someone on the street is sick. She is such a great cook, I know they all love her and want to return the favor," Dad says, with a proud smile on his face.

It's now after the usual lunch service, so the selection is limited but we find some wrapped sandwiches and salads and find a table near the window. Claire steps out to check a message and not wanting to leave Dad alone, I wait to check mine when she returns.

"When can the kids come for a visit this summer, Grace?" Dad asks.

"I think they will be free at the end of June. I told the girls they need to ask for a few days off so we can all come visit and get in some time at the lake with you and Mom," I answer.

"Well, you girls don't need to be at the lake before me and my little fishing buddy get there. This is the year. We are going to catch the big one," Dad says with a smile.

"Oh, I know! And let me tell you, he is excited. We were just talking about that the other night," I say. Since Dad only had daughters, he has always had a special place in his heart for my son. And he is larger than life in Seth's opinion too.

Claire returns and I excuse myself to make some calls. I step outside on the patio area because the hospital intercom is paging some doctors to one of the nursing floors and it's hard to hear. I call my boss and then Sophia, giving them an update about Mom's condition. They assure me that everything is being handled at work and for me not to worry. I am so thankful for both of them and tell them how much I appreciate their support. I don't know how people get through tough times if their boss isn't supportive. I feel very blessed to work for a great company.

The kids should be home now, so I give them a call. They are all there and act pretty happy to hear from me. I ask if they have talked to their dad and my oldest tells me he is on his way home. I decide to let him contact me. After this morning, I don't know if I can handle hearing his voice. The girls are working on dinner and Seth is taking out the trash and feeding the dog. Normal, everyday life. I suddenly miss them so much. I tell them I will probably be home in a day or two since Grandma seems to be doing better. We say I love you and good-bye for now. There's no message on the app or email from Andrew, but I know he said he was conducting a training exercise today and wouldn't be available. I smile, thinking of him, in his flight suit commanding his team. I love thinking of him. It's such a comfort to me anytime, but especially now. He has been so supportive and isn't even here.

When I return to the café, Dad and Claire have finished eating and start gathering their trash. We are going back upstairs to see if Mom feels like visiting or would rather rest. When we get off the elevator, we can see the door to Mom's room. Nurses and other staff are moving quickly in and out and we can see the emergency cart just inside the door. I grab Dad's arm and he just stares straight ahead not believing his eyes.

CHAPTER 25

My mind is racing. Being in the medical field, we all know there is a thing called knowing too much. I need to get Dad and Claire to a private area and try to find out what happened.

"Claire, please get Dad to this waiting area around the corner. It will be a little quieter for you two. I'll go see what's going on," I say, turning them in the direction of the waiting area. Fortunately, it's empty so at least they will have some privacy. Dad hasn't spoken at all, but that's okay, because I don't want to give him the scenario I think has happened.

The nurses' station is unoccupied. I hear call buttons ringing in the other rooms on the floor, so I'll just have to wait if I stay here. I head to Mom's room, hoping to see a familiar face or at least someone who can give me information.

There are too many people and too much equipment for me to enter the room so I'm only hearing information passed between the hospital staff. Respiratory therapy is attempting to place an airway, so I know it's bad. I hear them say they've entered an order for a CT of her head, so I think she is showing signs of a stroke. I'm trying to get the attention of her nurse, but she is straightening IVs and getting Mom ready for transport to Radiology.

"Is there anything I can do to help? I'm her daughter. You are going to CT, right?" I raise my voice over the rapid movement and talking. My voice sounds surprisingly calm to me given the situation. I feel like I'm watching everything happen in slow motion, like I'm watching a scene in a TV drama.

Mary, Mom's nurse, looks up and sees me in the doorway. "Oh Grace, honey. Let me get over to you," she says, shuffling past people and equipment to get to me, now outside the room.

"Mary, what happened? Did she have a stroke?" I ask, starting to feel myself come back to reality.

"Oh honey, I think so. She was resting a little after you all went to the cafeteria. The lab tech came in to draw her blood and couldn't get her to wake up. He called for me right away; and when I came in the room your mom had vomited and was having some seizure activity. Her face is drooping a little on the right side and she isn't responding to our commands. We will get her CT scan done quickly to confirm and determine the extent," she explains.

The staff was bringing Mom's bed through the door and rushing her to the elevator. I said a prayer that Claire and Dad couldn't see her from the waiting room.

"Mary, will you mind speaking to Dad and Claire? I don't know if I can hold it together right now," I say. I am starting to feel the adrenaline making me shake and the reality of this is starting to hit hard.

"Yes, I will do that now. Do you need a minute before you see them?" she asks.

"No, I need to be there. They are in the small waiting room behind the elevators," I say, as we begin walking in that direction.

Mary does a superb job explaining and answering their questions. She holds Dad's hand for a little bit and tries to reassure us all. She gives me her pager number and the extension at the nurses' station. She says she is going to check on the progress and will be back to keep us updated with every detail.

We sit in the waiting room, none of us knowing what say or where to look. We just sit, silent and helpless. There are no words of comfort or reassurance that I can find. In an instant, this changes everything for our family. I start to cry and look over at Dad. He is still, expressionless. I can't let him see me cry, I have to be strong for him. I take a few deep breaths and stand up, walking around the room. I see a coffee pot on a table by the windows. Yes, coffee, I'll make coffee. At least it's something to do. I must do something, anything…. then I hear it, over the hospital intercom, a page for the code blue team to Radiology. Then I know, this is the end for my beautiful mother. My dad and Claire look at me and they know it too.

"Girls, both of you, come over here right now. We are going to pray. We are going to pray for God's will, not our own. You know your mother always said that we should pray for God's plan. She said humans pray for the wrong things instead of God's will," Dad says, strong as ever but I can tell he's privately praying for a miracle.

We bow our heads and take turns praying, crying, and praying some more. We spend probably fifteen minutes begging God to wrap Mom in His arms and heal her, do His will, and give us peace. I don't think my prayer is sincere at all. I want to scream and beg God to give me my mother back. Just more time with her, I will do anything.

I look up in between sobs and see Mary and Mom's doctor approaching. The doctor sits beside Dad, expresses her sympathy and tells us that Mom has died. She suffered a massive cerebral hemorrhage, which they confirmed with the CT. Before the scan was complete, Mom stopped breathing and they attempted CPR, but she was gone. The doctor stays a bit longer and offers sympathy and clergy services. We decline the clergy services and express our thanks. She leaves us with her card and encourages us to call if we need to talk. Mary stays a bit longer with us. She has the gift of a nurse and tries to comfort and care for our broken hearts. But there's nothing she can do. There's nothing any of us can do. I have never felt so helpless and lost in all my life.

The three of us leave the hospital stunned. I had never imagined that my mother would die today or anytime soon. Even almost a year ago, when she called me to tell me she had cancer, I felt like she had a long life ahead. She was the center of our family. She always knew what to say and what to do. She always had time to listen. It feels like a hole has ripped through my chest.

None of us talked on the way to my parent's home. Claire took Dad inside and I decided to go to a few of their close neighbors and tell them the news. I don't want anyone to ask Dad about her and then he would have to explain. All the neighbors are as shocked as we were. We hug and cry, but there's nothing else to say. They express their sympathies and promise to be available for anything we need. I have known these good people nearly all my life. They loved Mom. I know as soon as the door closed, they were now organizing food, flowers, and whatever came to mind.

Standing in the driveway, I try to call my husband. Getting no answer, I send him a text to call me as soon as possible. I want to talk to him before I call the kids. He needs to be with them. I make a quick call to my boss and then Sophia, telling them I am not sure how long I'll be gone, depending on what needs to be done. Both assure me they will take care of everything.

I feel so helpless and lost. I feel like I should be doing something, but what? I can't fix this; I can't make everything all right like I always try to do. All I can do is stand here in front of my parent's home, helpless. I hardly recognize my reflection in the big window. My shoulders are slumped, and I look lost. I feel like I no longer belong here.

Mom's swing on the porch is swaying slightly in the breeze, making a faint squeak with each move. Dad installed that for her for Mother's Day a few years ago. It was (God, I hate past tense) her favorite place to relax when the weather was nice. I settle into it sideways, tucking my legs under me and lying my head on the back of the swing. The breeze swings me gently as I start to cry.

An hour later, my husband finally calls back. Like all of us, he is shocked. I ask him to put the kids on the phone so I can at least feel like I'm there with them. I need to be with them right now, even if it's just on the phone. Our hearts break together as a family. This is so hard and it's even worse telling them over the phone. I try to answer questions, but it is what it is. They will make phone calls to the school, neighbors, and friends and plan to drive here in the morning. Just knowing that I will see the kids soon is a comfort. I'm not sure how I feel about seeing my husband.

CHAPTER 26

It's almost dark now and Claire is sitting at the kitchen table with Dad. They both look as tired as I feel, and I sink into the chair next to Dad. In a soft voice, I tell them my family will be here tomorrow and that I talked to the neighbors who were home.

"Thanks, Grace. We made an appointment for tomorrow at the funeral home to decide on arrangements. I'd like both of you to go with me," Dad looks like he is about to break down.

"Would you both like to go for a walk? I know you said you aren't hungry Dad, maybe it will be good to get some fresh air," Claire asks, being helpful, as always.

"I think I'll just go lay down for a little bit. I might feel like a sandwich later," Dad says as he rises from his chair and heads to his room.

I wait until I hear Dad's door close. "I'll go with you, if you want to take a walk, Claire. I need to be doing something. I feel like I can't breathe, and I am going to just sit and cry if I don't get moving," I say.

"Let's go. I need it too. This is the worse day of my life. I feel numb, like it isn't real, Grace. What are we going to do without her? What is Dad going to do?"

"I don't know. One step at a time, I guess. We need to think about what Mom would want. I don't know if she and Dad ever talked about it. Let's get outside, these walls are suffocating me."

Later that night, we all force ourselves to eat something. After dinner, Claire hears from Scott; he is going to fly in tomorrow night. Dad makes some calls to cousins and mom's brother. All live within the metro area and said they will come over either tomorrow or the next day. The kids had a video call with us and spent quite a bit of time talking to Dad. They have no idea how much that helped him and helped me too. I can't wait to see them.

With nothing else to do, I shower and go to bed early but of course, couldn't sleep. I'm really on edge about seeing my husband tomorrow. He knows I heard that woman in the background when we were on the phone. It's not as if our marriage hasn't been strained and awkward, but I should have seen it before now. Have there been other women? No, I don't want to know the answer to that. Was it going on since he hired her? Or did he see opportunity since I was gone? Should I just act like it didn't happen and deal with it later? Whatever. I don't care. I'm tired of trying to be the perfect wife, mother, everything. I am sick of trying so hard. I wish Andrew was here. I love how he makes me feel. I can escape whenever I talk to him. I need him. I can't deal with this.

"Andrew, are you there?" I type into the app. I wait a bit, reading the news and scrolling through some social media but he isn't there. I decide to just tell him, he'll see it when he is free. "Andrew, Mom passed away today. It was a terrible shock to all of us. We will make funeral arrangements tomorrow. Sorry to tell you this way. I hope you are safe. Write if you can."

In the morning, I am disappointed that I don't have a message from Andrew. He is the one person I really want to talk to right now.

After forcing ourselves to eat a light breakfast, we are early for our appointment at the funeral home. We sit there numb as the funeral director rambles on about casket finishes, interiors, vault choices, headstones, on and on. Good lord, I think, who had any idea? Does it matter? I want to scream at him, "Does it really matter? She's gone!" Instead, I just nod and agree with whatever Dad and Claire choose. Trying not to cry, I mumble, "That will be lovely" when they make decisions.

Choosing songs is even harder but Dad selects some classics that Mom liked. The directors ask us to bring clothes for Mom and suggest styles that work well for funerals. That's it! I have to excuse myself, almost running out of the building. I can't do this! I hear Claire say she will take care of that and bring clothes by later today.

I am trying to catch my breath between tears when I get to the parking lot. I have to get control of myself and be strong for Dad. I lean forward and put my hands out to steady myself on Claire's rental car and try to stop crying. Just breathe, I tell myself. Get it together. I need to be strong for Dad and I'm falling apart.

I feel my Dad's arms around me. "Grace, it's okay. Let it out. Just cry, you need to cry."

I lean into Dad's strong arms and let it all out. I am bawling like a baby. I can't help it; my chest hurts so bad. I have never felt pain like this. I just want it to stop. I want my mother. How am I going to survive without her? I'll never see her again or hear her kind voice. She is gone! I can't believe she is gone. I think about my children and start crying even harder. They need her just as much I do.

Dad just holds me as I cry. I try to talk but I'm sure he can't make out a word I'm saying. He strokes my hair and tries to comfort me, but nothing can. She is gone. My beautiful mother is gone. Dad just lets me be human. He feels so strong. I feel like a little girl in his arms, but he can't make this pain go away. For once, I can't make everything okay for everyone around me. He just lets me grieve.

I have completely ruined his shirt, which Dad laughs about, then he says gently to me, "Grace, your mother told me the last time you visited that you were unhappy." I start to open my mouth to reassure him, say everything is fine. "Stop. You and Claire never could lie to your mother and I've picked up on that gift of hers over the years too. Your faces always told the truth. I know something is going on. Your husband couldn't stay off his phone long enough to have a conversation when you were here. I know what that means. He doesn't have much of a poker face either. I'm not here to say anything negative about him. I've loved him like a son and always will. But you deserve to be happy. Life is too short to be with someone who can't make you happy. You don't have to put up the perfect façade for everyone else and be miserable. I support whatever you need to do, baby. The timing of all this is terrible, but you are strong. Claire, your kids, and I will be with you all the way. Do you understand me?"

I start crying all over again and Dad cries with me for everything we've lost in the last few days.

CHAPTER 27

The day of the funeral arrives and passes like a blur. We are all so busy receiving kind words and condolences from family and friends, that there isn't any time to stop and think. The children are wonderful. Scott and my husband are perfect gentlemen. The funeral is a beautiful tribute to a beautiful woman. My boss and secretary drove 4 hours together to attend the service and Claire's firm sent gorgeous flowers. I felt so blessed with so many loving friends and family around us.

We decide to stay another day to be sure Dad was okay. We all help to write the thank you notes and eat some of the wonderful food neighbors had provided. Dad was doing fairly well. He planned some rounds of golf with his buddies and talked to the pastor about getting back into a Bible study class. Claire and Scott were going to fly back Sunday night and have a few days at home before returning to work. We said our goodbyes Sunday morning. We had to drive separately since I had come when Mom went to the hospital. The girls rode with me and the boys followed behind.

Driving home was hard. Since the funeral, I could not think about Mom without bursting into tears. But sometimes I was able to have a little smile when I remembered something I loved about her. The girls were busy on their phones and talking like they always do in the car. I just sat back and drove, letting the road soothe my mind. I thought of Andrew. I hadn't had any messages from him since Mom died. I'm little surprised by that. I didn't think he would be unable to write, but I guess things can change quickly in his position. It's okay though, since I honestly don't know what else to say to him about her death. I think I just need to get back to my routine. Just put my life on autopilot while I heal.

When we get home and unpack, it's late afternoon. The kids are in their rooms, on their phones checking in with friends. I'm in my bedroom, organizing clothes for the week when my husband comes in.

"Grace, I know we need to talk. If you would rather wait, that's fine. I just want you to know I'm ready when you are," he says.

My stomach suddenly feels like it's in a knot. I don't know if I can do this. How can he want to talk about this when I just buried my mother? I can't believe his nerve. From the look on his face, it's obvious that he isn't going to apologize and want to start fresh with a focus on us. Clearly, there isn't any good outcome for me by waiting, so I might as well hear what he has to say.

"Go ahead, I'm listening," I say softly, not making eye contact.

"Let's sit down at least," he says, guiding me to the two sitting chairs I have near the window. This is one of my favorite spots to read, but I don't think it will be a favorite spot for me after today.

"Grace, you and I both know we have drifted apart over the past year or so," he begins, "I have felt like I don't hold an important place in your life anymore. You have worked so hard to get to the position you have in your company and I feel like that comes first with you. Then the kids, the house, everything else. I have felt like you didn't have time for me anymore. So, I poured myself into my work. It's the only thing I could do when I don't get any attention at home," he looks at me for a reaction, stopping for a moment.

I keep my composure, even though this is ridiculous, surely this isn't what he is telling himself. "Go on," I say, glancing up at him, then looking at my lap.

"I know this isn't a good time for you, but I think I should move out for a little while so we both have some time to think through this," he says, looking like a total schmuck.

"Really…. And what do you think that will accomplish? How would that help us work on our problems if you are somewhere else?" I ask, trying not to raise my voice.

"I just think it will help both of us to be able to focus and reflect on what we really want in life," he says.

Now I lose it.

"You mean it will help you to focus on your secretary's naked body underneath you! You mean you don't need the distraction of your family to get in the way of that. So, you can reflect on what you really want. Really?? If you want to go, then go, you haven't been here for me either.

I hope you remember that! Take a good look at that king size bed where I've slept alone! But, right, you are saying that I was focused on my career and didn't have time for you. Funny, I have been right where you left me, when you chose to sleep in your office, or the den, or with your secretary!"

"I'm going to go tonight, Grace. You can reach me on my cell if you need me. I'll check on the kids tomorrow," he says, pausing for a second at the door.

"Really? You are leaving me to tell the kids by myself?" I scream at him.

"They already know, Grace. They are teenagers, I already talked to them," he says.

"How could you do that? You didn't even talk to me! We are separating and I'm the last to know?? That's fantastic, just great. Did you ever once think to ask me how I feel?" I am struggling to talk through the tears streaming down my face. After the past week, how is it possible that I have any tears left? How is it possible that I've lost my husband and my mother in a matter of days?

"No, I didn't ask how you felt. I'm sorry Grace. I think I should go now; I'll give you some time, call me if you need anything," he says walking out the door.

I stand there, awestruck by his arrogance. If I need anything?? I "needed" a husband who loved me, you idiot. My body crumples into what is now my least favorite chair in this huge house. I hear him say goodbye to the kids, and then the door to garage shutting. I feel like never moving again, I just want to die. I feel deflated, empty.

"Momma?" the kids open the door just a crack. "Can we come in?"

"Yes babies, come in," I wipe my face and moving to the bed so we can all sit together.

"Sorry about you and Dad," Seth says, the girls nodding and echoing his words, each finding a spot near me on the bed.

"Yeah, I am too, baby," I say, pulling him into my arms.

"It will be okay, Mom. It will all work out, don't worry," Sarah says.

"Yes, I know. We will all be okay, you are right. Let's cuddle up here and watch some Netflix or something, get our minds on something else for a while," I move the pillows around until everyone finds a spot.

Halfway through some corny movie we have all seen probably twenty times, I look over and the girls are asleep. Seth is not far from drifting off too. I pull the blankets around them, turn the tv volume down and give them all some extra room by curling up in my reading chair nearby. I lean my head back and say a prayer, thanking God for what I have left, my children, my sister, and my dad. I say a little prayer for Andrew too.

CHAPTER 28

In the morning, even though the pain from losing Mom is still so real, I decide I can't stay in this house. Everywhere I look causes me to think of my husband. So, I call my boss and tell him I am coming into the office. He insists there is no reason for me to come in because he has everything covered. He tells me to take some more time for myself. But after my protesting and promising I'll leave if I need to, he relents and tells me to do what I want.

Sophia fills me in on the events of last week and gives me an agenda for the day. It's pretty full, even for a Monday and being off last week, but I am glad of that. I can decide which meetings I want to attend since everything thinks I am out of the office. But, I need to keep my mind busy and off my husband. He hasn't called since he left last night, and I don't expect to hear from him. I don't know what I'd say to him anyway. I think this is really it, my marriage is over. Glancing at some reports on my desk, I see the picture of us taken on vacation in Mexico about five years ago. I quickly grab it and stuff it one of the desk drawers before my tears have a chance to start again.

"Grace?" Sophia says over the phone intercom, "There's a delivery for you. Can I bring it in your office?"

"Yes, please do. Do I need to sign for it?" I ask.

She is already at the door with the most amazing floral arrangement I have ever seen in my life. I have never seen anything so beautiful or exotic. I don't even recognize some of the flowers.

"Wow, this is gorgeous! The card is clipped on the side. Do you need me to get you any more water for it or do you want any coffee for yourself?" she asks, not prying as to who it is from which is one of the many things I love about her.

"No, no, I'm good. That is so beautiful. Thank you so much for bringing it in. This brightens up the entire room!" I say.

"Yes, it really does! Oh, I hear the phone, let me know if you need anything," she smiles as she closes the door behind her.

This flower arrangement is outstanding. I recognize a few of the flowers in it, the orchids and calla lilies at least. There are spikes of aloe vera too. I would have never thought to ask for those in a bouquet, but they bring an exotic, almost tropical feel to it. I google a few of the others and learn they are Bird of Paradise, celosia, and yellow trumpet. It's gorgeous. I take the card out of the small envelope, wondering who in the world sent this work of art.

Dear Grace,
My deepest sympathies to you and your family. I am in your service; whatever need may arise.
All my love,
Andrew

Wow, I can't believe he did this! This is the most thoughtful gesture; I am in shock. I haven't even talked to him since Mom died. I pick up my phone and send him a heartfelt thank you through the app. It's night there so I might catch him in his room.

"Grace, there is no need to thank me, I wanted to do something, anything. I'm furious that I can't be there with you as you grieve."

As I read, his words surround me. I physically feel warm, like I'm being held.

"Andrew, you have no idea what this means to me. What you mean to me. This has been a very hard time for me, just awful. Knowing that you are here makes all the difference," I type.

"I will always be here, Grace. No matter what happens, miles cannot keep me away from you. Don't forget that. You are my queen, my one love. I must go now. I will write you when I can. Stay safe."

Before I can respond, he is gone. I wish we could have talked. There is so much I want to tell him. I don't know if I'm ready to tell him about my separation or not. Only the kids know. I will call Claire and Dad tonight. I just can't face it, honestly, the reality hasn't sunk in. I certainly can't talk about it without crying. I just need some time. It's hasn't even been a full day since he left and I dread the rest of the week, each day emphasizing that my marriage is most likely over. As lonely as I felt when he was in our home, I feel even lonelier now. The children left this morning about fifteen minutes before I did. In that short span of time, the silence was deafening. The clock seemed so loud I could feel every tick reverberate in my ears. I couldn't stay, I had to leave. Is that what it will be like when the children are gone to college or off to start their own lives? I don't know if I can stand it.

Shaking off that thought, I rise from my office chair and walk around the room stopping at the table. The floral arrangement is so beautiful, Sophia positioned it perfectly on the small conference table by the bookcase. Mom would have loved it. She was a passionate gardener. Andrew never met her, but he sent a perfect tribute to her beautiful life. I start to cry. I let the tears come. They must come, I tell myself, so eventually I will be okay.

CHAPTER 29

Almost a week has passed since my husband moved out. He has been back to our home to get personal belongings twice and visit with the kids. He says he hasn't found an apartment yet and is just staying at the office and using the workout room showers. I doubt that is true, but I think it's better I don't know, so I don't ask. He has opened a bank account and moved some funds over for his new expenses. We decide to leave both our names on our joint accounts, and both commit to covering the house and other expenses like we always have until we decide what the future holds. I still have my own personal account, my "mad money" as Mom called it. He doesn't know it exists and I'm glad to have it. Mom always gave good advice and here is more evidence of her wisdom.

Dad and Claire are both incredibly supportive, as I knew they would be. Claire has spoken with her boss and they have an attorney in the firm who is licensed to practice in Nebraska. She promises to be available whenever I'm ready or if I just want advice. She and Scott both promise to come help with the kids or just be here at a moment's notice. Dad offers to come as well and plans to take Seth for a weeklong fishing trip next month. Seth is excited and the girls are jealous. They both have already committed to their summer jobs though. Seth is glad he will have Granddad all to himself.

Life is starting to feel a bit more routine. Honestly, there are times that I miss my husband but more times that I don't. I don't miss trying to guess what his mood will be, if he will look my way, guessing when he will get home (often much later than I hoped), or if he has eaten—should I prepare something or not? Do I have time to go for a run or will he be pulling in the driveway as I'm leaving? Do I wait up or can I get some much-needed sleep? Yeah, I'm definitely leaning toward not missing him. I know I am grieving not just my mother, but the loss of being married. There is something secure about marriage, as lonely as it was, that made me feel whole, part of something. That's what I miss the most, not him.

On Friday afternoon, I'm in my office wrapping up the week when my boss calls me to his office. "Grace, how are you doing? You seem to be okay but are you really?" he asks.

"Yes, I think so. I have my moments, but it helps to be busy and occupied. How have you been?" I ask, knowing that he just finished a brutal budget planning retreat, going head to head with the other VPs for resources for their new pharmaceutical products that received FDA approval recently and are preparing to go to market.

"Good, good, no worries. I'm fine, glad to have you back," he says, taking a big drink of coffee. I don't think I've ever seen him drink anything but coffee. No matter the time of day, he always is drinking coffee. "You know there's the annual pharmaceutical conference in a few months. It's being held in Montreal this year."

"Yes, I know it is nearly time for it again," I say. This is the annual conference to report on new drugs and technologies, and the business side of pharmaceuticals. I am a licensed PharmD but I really love the financial reporting and marketing. I usually attend this conference for those sessions specifically.

"We have an opportunity to share our results with the line of opioid mixed agonists, both clinical and financial. I thought you would be the perfect presenter," he says, looking at me with a face that tells me I don't get to say no.

"I would be honored to do that. Opioid addiction is a worldwide issue and we should showcase our efforts to address the problem while still treating the patient's pain. I know that session will be well attended," I answer.

"Great, prepare your slides and data and we will review them, say in a month? Then you'll have time to adjust and finalize things in time for us to submit it to the conference for the agenda planning. Let me know if you need any help," he says, turning back to his work.

"Thanks, I will. And thank you for everything and coming to the funeral, I really appreciate it," I say as I turn to leave his office.

"Of course, Grace, don't mention it. I'm here if you need anything and I mean that sincerely," he says, softening a little. "Have a good weekend. Tell the kids hello."

Interesting that he didn't say 'tell your husband and the kids hello' or 'tell your family hello". Maybe I was the only one who didn't see my marriage ending.

CHAPTER 30

I work a little bit longer until I reach a good stopping point for the weekend. As I am locking my office door, my phone rings. It's my bank. That's odd, why would they call at almost five pm on a Friday?

"Hello, Grace? This is John Stowe at the bank. Do you have a second to talk?"

"Sure, sure, John, let me step back into the office here. I was just locking up. Ok, what's going on? Is there a problem?" I ask, moving to my chair. I have a funny feeling from the tone of his voice that I need to be sitting.

"Grace, I know your husband moved some funds to another account recently," he begins. "And that's not what this is about. You have an account that only has your name on it."

"Yes, that's correct. I've had it since before I got married," I answer, "Why?"

"Well, there have been some odd withdrawals from that account. We have no one else listed on the account. Is there anyone who you may have given access?"

"No, my sister knows I have it, but she doesn't know which bank or any details. Mom advised both of us years ago to set up a private account just in case we needed it," I explain.

"That's good advice. Does your sister live in the US?" he asks, making me even more nervous.

"Yes, in New York. She has lived there for many years now," I answer.

"Well, these are small amounts, a thousand here, a few hundred the next time, but they are going somewhere overseas but when we ping that transaction, it's like it goes nowhere. The first withdrawal was about 90 days ago, the most recent is today."

"What does this mean? Is my money gone?" I feel like I can't breathe. "Have any of our joint accounts been touched?"

"No, everything on those appear fine. I know tomorrow is Saturday, but I'd like you to come in and look at this with me. Is 9 am too early? If these are fraudulent, then you are protected, and the bank will reimburse you for unauthorized withdrawals, minus a liability limit as defined by the FDIC. We will work with you, Grace; you have been a long-time customer and we will help take care of this."

"I don't check that account often, but I had just over fifty thousand in it. How much is missing?" I ask, bracing for his answer.

"Just under fifteen thousand. There have been quite a number of withdrawals, all have been a thousand or less, so the amounts didn't send up any major red flags, it was the frequency that trigged an internal audit. And then the money going overseas is a big question mark for us, so that's why I wanted to talk to you," John explained.

"Ok, thank you so much, I'm glad you caught it and called me. I'll be at your office in the morning. Thanks again, John," I say as we hang up.

I am completely stunned. I can't ask my husband; he didn't even know about this account anyway. John didn't act like he thought he was the one making the withdrawals anyway. Suddenly, my heart sinks as I look over at the arrangement from Andrew. I have a terrible feeling. I know who did this. Pulling out my phone, I stare at the pictures Andrew sent from the media interview and his profile picture. I stare at them for a moment, not sure if I want to know the truth. With everything going on with my family, I forgot about the pictures Andrew sent to me. I google a reverse image search site and drop one of the pictures into the site's search bar. I wait, my heart beating so hard I feel the throbbing in my ears.

"Retired Lieutenant James Addison-Davies speaks at the 2013 Royal Climate Conference". I read the entire article, the whole damning evidence that the person I loved is not real. Anger crawls up my spine and into my entire body. How could he? My hands shaking, I copy the web result and click it into our chat and type my goodbye, tears of anger and pain streaming down my face.

"Stay away from me."

CHAPTER 31

Immanuel

What a great morning! Praise God! My life was filled with negativity but no more! I shower and dress, putting on some of my best clothes. Although, I smile to myself, thanks to many generous clients, all my clothes are my best. Life is good, oh yes, life is good! I will someday use my good fortune to rise above and no longer be bound to this demeaning work. I don't like doing this, but what other choice is there for me? My passion is real estate and wealth management. Although one would have to be born into the business or be very lucky to break into those businesses here. All I can do keep trying, keep hustling. When one has enough money, then all the opportunity one would want rains down.

After a quick cup of tea and some fruit for breakfast, I back my Mercedes out of the drive. It is ten years old but is an upgraded model and gets me respect. That's what it is all about. Showing what I have, what my intelligence has brought me. Not what my country brings anyone, that is nothing but despair, certainly there are no jobs for men like me here. When something comes open, it is given to the relative of someone in government or whoever can bribe their way into the job. Nothing like that comes to men like me. I won't be part of that corruption anyway; I will do things my way. I will only answer to God and myself.

Life has been kind lately. Many clients have contributed to help me, most graciously I must say. They hear the stories I tell of misfortunate, illness, or crisis and respond quickly to help. That's what friends do, right? Even when you don't know the real person you have a connection with, you are still connected. Still human. That's the great thing about middle age or older women (and men for that matter), they are all looking for one more chance at love. To be young again. I give them that gift, it's what they want. If they didn't, they wouldn't be on dating websites, searching, seeking, waiting to find Mr. Right. I'll be your Mr. Right. I'm happy to help you with that, my beautiful friend. Later, when I feel the time is right, you will help me. I smile to myself. I can be very persuasive, but honestly, I've never had to work that hard, the clients are usually putty in my hands. If they are resistant, I have other ways to get the funds I need from them. I am discrete, it isn't the amount one pulls from an individual. Businessmen like me have many clients and rarely do any of them notice small amounts missing here and there.

I drive along the coast, my sunglasses on, the window down, enjoying this day in my young life. I'm not actually sure how old I am. I think around thirty, which is getting a bit old in this business. My mother died when I was a very young child and my father was often called away. The older children at the primary school teased me that he couldn't stay home because he was called away by drink and strange women. Either way, he didn't have time for me and now I don't have time for him. He has tried to contact me, but I won't have that negativity around me. Life is too good. I was raised by a woman who I called my Auntie, but I really don't think she was related to me. She was just a kind soul in my village. She became late from malaria; I think it was two years ago already. I can't dwell on the past now, and certainly not that old fashioned village where poverty hangs around one's neck like a noose. And not while I drive my luxury car and live my blessed life. If only those older boys in the village could see me now.

As I drive, I'm thinking fondly about all the clients who have helped me, and how I've helped them. It's a good thing to feel loved and desired, is it not? I like talking to them. It's mostly European women that I target. They are my best clients. I don't know why European women are so lonely, it must be the cold. I would never live in a cold place; it must cloud one's thinking. I need the sunshine on my skin to feel alive. A few European men, too, I just adjust the persona I adopt, no big deal. Men usually have more money and are more generous with it. They like to feel like they are saving the damsel in distress. My brothers and I can play the lover in distress very well. My second favorite clients are Asian woman. They are almost always financially secure enough to be very generous. They have proven over and over that their generosity is just who they are as a culture. They often don't even question the details of a request. They are just quick to help. They are unlike Americans most of whom aren't generous, although I enjoy them very much. They are a bit more challenging; it all looks good until I ask for money. Then I see their feelings for me aren't as deep as they say. But I persist and usually win in the end.

I smile at my reflection in the rear-view mirror as I cruise along. This life looks good on me. I am going to the bar to watch my football team on TV. A few friends will be there, and we can have a few bottles and enjoy life today.

I tried a new approach recently and am pleased with my progress but not in a financial way. This one is different. I found a beautiful woman on a professional website in America. Her name is Grace. She is so incredibly intelligent; she turns me on so much just talking to her. I fantasize about watching her in a board room, conducting business, and making deals. She loves to read, debate any topic, especially economics and business, with me. She challenges my intellect; I have to read many of our chats and emails twice just to be sure I understand all the concepts and terms she uses. I like to read our conversations over and over anyway, I love everything about her. Sometimes she says I challenge her intellect too. I like that, I want her to know I'm smart and to be interested in the same things I am. She is a mother, a successful businesswoman, everything in a woman I pray to God to give me. She is married though and made it very clear to me that she won't leave her husband.

I am falling for her, I know that. I can't help it. She is still my client at this point, but I want her to be my girl. I wish I could think of a way for her to know the real me and love me, Immanuel, not Andrew. We could build a life together and I could leave my past behind.

When we started talking, I had every intention for her to be my client. I sent her the standard links under the ruse of love songs and other romantic sites to set up various ways to pull money when the time is right. I always do that in the event that the client doesn't have the level of sympathy to send help when I ask. All that changed quickly though, as we talked, I knew I would never do that her. She is different from any woman I have ever known. In my business we never work completely alone, but I won't share her with anyone. My business partners have asked me, even begged me, for her contact information and to let them talk to her. I won't; she is special. They warn me that I should be careful, and they swear she'll be ruthless if she discovers the truth. I'll protect her from them and keep her to myself. Maybe someday, I'll be able to tell her who I really am. She is such a loving, kind woman, maybe God will make a way for her to forgive me, understand what it's like here, and love the real me.

CHAPTER 32

I park my car outside the sports bar. The game has already started but that's okay. I'm here to talk about some deals with my friends also. We work together and help one another out. I have to keep relationships strong in business and be on the front edge. There is no hope for success if one is the last to know. I am always researching and learning while I wait for my big break to get out of here. The more I know about everything, the less chance someone can take advantage of me. That is true in any business, but even more in my business. I must always be present and prepared. I have a strong belief in that. It will pay off someday for me.

"Immanuel! Over here, we are waiting for you. How bodi-? Wetin dey happen o?" they greet me in Pidgin English.

"How far? Wetin dey?" I answer. "Make we go shayo, then talk o!"

The bartender sees my hand and brings my two friends, Amobi and Enofe their usual bottles and my whiskey and water. We always come here when the game is on, so the bartender knows our order. The cable and the electricity can't be trusted in our homes. The grid will shut off just when you are watching at home or doing something important. Sometimes it does here too, but businesses have a better chance.

I take a sip of my drink and it burns my throat. This is a better drink than a bottle, my friends don't know they need to show better quality when out in public. One should always be known as having good taste for the finer things in life. I know what I want and usually how to get it. I won't rest until I get the best of everything, but they like to play and have fun. Their focus is sometimes lacking. Not me, I live and breathe to gain more knowledge and get the best life. I don't want what is available around me, I want what the world can offer.

"When are you going to let us talk to the American woman, Immanuel? You need to share her with your friends" Amobi says, laughing. "Are you afraid I am too good, and she will love me more?"

"Sharrap ya dirty mouth! Never! She is too good to talk to you! True to God! No more words about her!" I stare at Amobi until he looks away. Then I glare at Enofe so he understands too. I will not tolerate this talk from them.

They turn to talking business that I'm not interested in. Minor things, like mail order and delivery scams. I don't like that; I want to use my mind for better things. I go back to watching the game and people in the bar while they talk. I always like knowing my surroundings. One must be alert to influencers around you; the people who can help you in business. Everyone here is hustling, and one just must find the right opportunity. Glancing at my phone, I see there is a message waiting for me from Grace. I can't help but smile, I'm eager to know what it says. I won't open it here, not in this place, not around these people. I would never bring her here and always will always shield her from this side of me. I'll look at the message when I get home. It will be afternoon here when I get home, so late morning for her. Maybe she will be free and can chat.

Amobi and Enofe talk business with me. They are trying some new dating websites to see what type of clients are to be found. We review the balances of some accounts we share in common and the deposits of some recent pulls. I give them a monthly check from these accounts to cover the cost of their internet fees and other expenses. We have to spread the funds out across accounts. The banks should never know anyone's total assets. We don't need any eyes on our business.

The game ends, and my team lost by one. They did not play well, so they deserve to lose in my opinion. Don't show up if you aren't going to do your best, in sports or in business. Good things don't just happen, you have to give it all. I unlock my car and cruise back to my home, enjoying the warm day and looking forward to reading her message.

I pull my car through the gate to my home, watching in the rear-view mirror that it closes and locks out the world on the street. This is my sanctuary. I've had it meticulously landscaped with frangipani trees, plumeria, large aloe vera, and orchids. Very few people enter my estate, as I like to think of it, but those who are invited in receive a pleasant first impression.

Appearance is everything in business. My potential business contacts must know that I am able manage my home and my professional life with ease. I must give them no doubts about me, and I must be extremely careful about the few people I allow to be close to me.

Inside, I get comfortable in my office that overlooks the back garden. I pour another whiskey and water from my small office bar. One should keep a little when there is something to celebrate or business to discuss. A message from Grace is the perfect reason to celebrate. Now, to see what my love has for me today. I open our chat, smiling to myself and thinking of her.

One line followed by a link with the pictures I sent of my persona at the conference changes my entire life, "Stay away from me."

Oh fuck, what is this? I feel like I've been punched in my stomach. She knows. She found the pictures of the old white guy online. I'm so stupid! I should have known she would keep digging, doing research. She isn't stupid like the desperate clients on the dating sites. I made a rookie mistake. I was too arrogant! I let my feelings overtake common sense…Damn, I'll never get her back! I throw my glass across the room and it shatters as it hits the door frame. What am I going to do? I must think, there must be a way to explain this that she will believe. My head is pounding. Searching through my desk drawer I find what I need to stop the pain. I throw a few of the pills into my mouth and choke them down.

CHAPTER 33

"How far, yeah?" I pick up the phone. It has been ringing all morning and I am tired of listening to it.

"Immanuel, man. Wetin de happen? I thought you was dead. No one has seen you in over a week man. Wahala? What trouble is on you?" It's Amobi, he is the one who has been ringing my phone, bothering me.

"Nothin' man, I don't want to say. Just let me be now," I tell him.

"I'm outside your house. Open the gate, brother," he says.

I sigh and walk to the wall control for the gate and let him in. If I don't, he will continue to torment me.

"Wetin de happen, Immanuel? We don know what is your struggle. You no well?"

He isn't going to stop talking until I tell him. First, I get him a bottle and a drink for myself.

"She's gone man. She knows. I dey ache so bad," I tell him, half laying on the sofa.

"Who, the American? What happened man?" Amobi sits forward on his chair. He appears to be slightly sympathetic but looking somewhat happy about my misfortune.

"She kept asking me for other pictures of me. The profile picture wasn't enough. I should have known. She was generous with her photos when I asked, and I wanted her to be happy. I sent her some and she found the guy's real name on some old news story. I am such an idiot. I know better than to do that and now, I'll never get her back," I couldn't even look at Amobi, but I knew he was enjoying this.

"Man, you better be careful. She is smart. I told you she will hunt you down," Amobi warned.

"I never took anything from her. I only told her I was someone else. I would never do anything to hurt her. I wanted to tell her the truth all along, but I couldn't. She would never want me," I say.

"Come on man, what do you think would happen? She will forgive and fall in love with you? Immanuel, you are getting soft. There's a whole world of women like her or better, with a lot of money that you could get. Get back to hustling, man, you have to fill your stomach, you can't worry about some American. She is already over you; that I can promise you," Amobi says, eyes darting around the room.

"What are you looking around for? Why did you come here?" I ask, glaring at him. He looks different to me. "Did you get new clothes? How did you get here?"

"Just a haircut man, cool off. I have ways of getting what I need too. I can get around the city. You aren't the only Yahoo boy with a brain. I need a laptop. Mine isn't working right. You just got a new one, let me have your old one," he asks.

"What happened to the extra one I let you borrow? Is that what isn't working? I thought you were just using it until you bought a new one. Now it isn't working, is that what you are saying?" I ask, knowing he has broken it in his stupidity. Amobi acts like a spoiled child, never taking care of anything. He will never be successful and that's a fact.

"O! Man, you knew that didn't have life left in it when you gave it to me. You should have just asked me to put it in the garbage for you, that's how good it was," he lies.

"Fine. It is over there, you know that, your eyes have been on it since you walked in. Take it and go," I say, very tired of his presence in my home. "And bring the old one back. I can fix it."

"Yeah, yeah, next time, if I remember," Amobi says. He tucks the laptop under his arm like the thief he is and heads to the door. "Get over her, Immanuel. You should pray to God she doesn't find you."

"I said go, Amobi, you are done with your business here," I don't even look up as he shuts the door. But I do watch out the window as he walks to the street and I press the control for the gate behind him. What is he driving? I don't remember him having a car. Idiot probably stole it here in town. He isn't smart enough to raise the money on his own.

I fix myself another drink and walk to the bathroom. Amobi said it's been weeks since anyone has seen me. That can't be. Looking back from the bathroom mirror, he may be right. My hair looks busy and yes, I stink. I look like hell came for me.

CHAPTER 34

After a hot shower, I don't feel any better but at least I look human. I find my phone where I laid it after Amobi's intruding visit. He's nearly right. I check the day and time; it's been 8 days since Grace's message. God, just the thought of her and my stomach is in pain. I have to do something. What can I do? Maybe she will have pity on me, show mercy. I just want to talk to her. I don't care if she screams at me, I just want to hear her voice. I had so many dreams of her! She could have been my salvation from this life. A woman can save a man with her love. I believe it. And I know Grace's love is that strong.

I make a bowl of garri with milk and sit on the couch to eat it. I stare at the wall slowly eating and thinking. I wonder what she is doing. Did she and her husband reunite? God, I can't stand to think of that. I would grab him by the throat. How can he be so lucky and not appreciate her? What a fool. I would treat her like a queen every day! I pick up my phone just to have something to look at other than the wall. I can't help it; like a moth to the flame, I open the app we used.

Grace: Last seen at… 8 days ago. I stare at the screen while I eat. At least I guess I'm eating; I can't even taste my food. Her last message is there: "Stay away from me." That's all. No chance for me to explain, beg forgiveness, nothing. She is just gone. Gone from me. I lost her.

I toss my phone aside and return my empty bowl to the sink. The kitchen is spotless except for my bowl and spoon. I can't help it, out of habit, I must wash them and put them away now. I run hot water and scrub them both with a towel and soap. I cannot stand an untidy home. It says to me that the person's mind is untidy too. I wouldn't want to do business with people like that. I wipe the counters, stove, and sink until I am satisfied with them. Right now, it feels like this is the only control I have.

With nothing else to do, I head to my office and open my laptop. Doing so makes me think of that idiot Amobi. How does one person ruin a laptop? I should have known I wasn't going to get it back. In this place, when someone borrows something, everyone knows they are asking you to give it to them. There just isn't enough to go around. Everyone is in want. That is why I work so hard. I must lift myself out, be prepared to leave if I must. I found someone that could help me to do that and I lost her. I could have helped her too. I could have made her happy, I would not ignore the most wonderful woman in the world like that stupid husband of hers does. I can't think about her now. I'll do some work, make some deals, then maybe something will come to me. I lay my head on my desk and pray to God for help. After a ten-minute prayer of promises and deals that God and I both know I can't keep, I log on to talk to some clients. I must keep hustling. That's the only way to live here.

Two more days pass and I haven't left my home. I have immersed myself in work, chatting with clients all hours of the day and night. I sleep for no more than two hours at a time. I tend to have these bursts of intense focus and energy, especially after a setback. I know when I have to refocus my efforts and I have always done that with ease. It takes a toll on my body and mind though. In my country, there is no other way to get what I need. Hustle, hustle, hustle, make deals, then repeat.

CHAPTER 35

It's midnight. My phone buzzes on the desk next to my laptop. I glance at it but pause to get a glass of water before seeing who it is. I need to stretch my legs for a few minutes also. I've been sitting too long. A couple of deals have paid off nicely this week. I'll have a bit more money to save toward meeting my goals. Whatever my goals are now, I'm not sure. A little more than a week ago, I wanted to leave Africa and be with Grace. Now that doesn't seem to ever be a possibility. I haven't spent any time trying to think of a way to get her back. Every time she crosses my mind, my heart breaks all over again.

I stand outside on the balcony overlooking my back terrace and garden and sip my glass of water. The night is warm without any breeze. I'm barefoot, wearing shorts and a white linen shirt unbuttoned to try to stay cool. Grace would have liked this terrace. She was so pleased with the flowers I sent her when her mother passed. She appreciates the beautiful things in life. She is a classic beauty, always a lady, my queen. I smile, thinking of her. There must be a way for us. God wouldn't have been so cruel to a mere mortal to show me the perfect woman, then suddenly rip her away, never to speak again. I must keep the little hope I have that I will speak to her again.

I almost forgot my phone message. I get settled in my office and pick it up, expecting a routine client message, blah, blah, blah, how was your day? The usual boring chatter that gets me toward my purpose. It's not a client though. My heart jumps and I nearly drop my phone. It's Grace.

"You know by now; I know you aren't who you say you are. So, who are you? Why are you doing this to me? I suspected it all along, but I'm not happy I was right.

"I wasn't going to jeopardize my marriage for you or anyone else. It seems that my marriage has enough trouble on its own. I just enjoyed talking to someone who liked books, finance, economics, etc. as much as I do. And let's face it, you weren't going to show up one day and be madly in love with me. You never were. And that's fine, in a way, I knew it. Life is weird how it brings people into your life that you instantly connect with. I thought we were like kindred spirits.

"Anyway, I want to thank you for introducing me to some new books and ideas. You gave me an inner confidence I didn't know I was lacking. You helped me believe in myself and my instincts again. I'm stronger having known you, whomever you are.

"When you called me, I couldn't place your accent, but the connection was bad. Don't worry, I'm not reporting you. That's not the type of person I am. You always seemed a bit sad in your communication or maybe lonely; but maybe I just want to console myself by believing that now.

"I enjoyed you, I enjoyed us. I felt what I really thought was love. Maybe it was. I don't know. The carpet was pulled out from under me. Now I can't trust that anything I experienced was real. It might have been all a dream. I just want you to know that I believe there is good in people and I believed in the good in you. And, yes, I still believe love exists. I hope you do too."

Oh my god, I can't believe this. I read it again. She doesn't sound like she wants to hunt me down and kill me, of course, I wouldn't blame her if she did. She is still online. She can see I've read her message. I don't know what to say. Me, of all people, who can talk to literally anyone, cannot form a response or even a comprehensible sentence to reply.

"You aren't going to say anything at all? I know you aren't shy. Go ahead. Say something….," Grace writes.

I smile. That's my Grace. Straight to the point, but in a way that is welcoming and gracious. She can draw out the shyest person and make them feel they are the most interesting person in the room. I read her message again. I'm still afraid to speak, but I am so thankful for a chance.

"Do you really believe everything you just wrote?" I type. It's lame, I know, but I have to inch forward; test the waters more before speaking too much. She is typing a reply while I'm praying, oh God, help me, how can I get her back?

"How can you ask me that? I have always been completely honest; you are the one spinning a web of lies. I felt closer to you than anyone in a long time. You shattered everything I thought we had. I have done more thinking and crying over you since I discovered the truth than I have for any man my entire life. I believe I knew all along in my heart you were too good to be true, but I couldn't give you up. I'm no longer angry, I just want you to understand how deeply you hurt me. I am a human being with feelings, that should mean something to you."

I still can't speak. I know I'm testing her patience, but I cannot think of anything to say that will help my case or ease the pain I've put her through.

"I think you need to start talking soon."

"What do you what from me?" I ask, cringing. God, it sounds like she is the one who deceived me. I feel like an awkward teenager, this is not going well.

"Nothing, I guess. I just wanted the chance to speak to you. The real you, not some persona, not some old, military general. Who are you?"

"It's me Grace, the same person you have been talking to all along. You know me, just not my circumstances. Please, tell me you have been okay. I was sick when you left, I deserved to die. I loved you. If I had known at the start what a beautiful, amazing woman you are, I never would have tried to deceive you. The more I learned about you, I was afraid to turn it around and come clean. I was afraid that you would be gone forever," I knew I was doing a poor job of explaining, but I had to speak, just to keep talking to you, anything.

"So, you just continued to create this fantasy? Keep stringing me along? Until when? Eventually you would have to come home. You would have to meet me. Your story couldn't continue forever," Grace typed.

"I know, Grace, I know. I am so sorry. I beg for your forgiveness. I fell in love; I was desperate to keep you. I wanted you to be mine. I know you probably won't believe me, but I still love you and always will. I wanted you so much that I preferred to keep the fake me than risk losing you if I told you the truth," I write.

"So, you are African, right?"

Her question stops me in my tracks. How would she know that? Or is she testing me?

"What do you mean?" I reply, dragging out any confession I may have to make.

"It's a pretty simple question. You live in Africa, right?"

"What makes you think that, Grace? Are you coming for me?"

"Well, it's clear, you are a romance scammer. A Yahoo boy, right? Does 419 mean anything to you? You know I love to read, so I've done quite a bit of reading about people like you," her words are cutting through me.

"Yes, I live in Africa," I confess.

"Thank you for confirming that. I think you owe me at least some information. Can I be completely honest with you?"

"Yes, please do, Grace," I am secretly urging her to keep talking to me. This is like salve on my soul. Deep within me, I need her to expose me, rip all the lies I've told away and reveal my secrets. I love her, I want her to see me, to bring salvation to my heart.

"I want to know your name, but I understand if you won't tell me. I am going to ask you some questions. I want you to be honest with me and if you can't answer, fine, just tell me you can't answer, ok?"

"Yes, I will be honest or silent, I promise," I answer.

"I loved you. I loved how kind and compassionate you were. You didn't judge me, even though I revealed plenty of my faults during the time we were talking. In fact, you didn't judge anyone, you'd say, "Well, that's for them to decide", never suggesting you knew better than another about how to live their life. You didn't pressure me to leave my husband or do something stupid. You never asked me for help, money or otherwise. Maybe you just didn't have the right opportunity yet. Was that it? You were waiting for the right time? Were you going to? Scam me, I mean?" Grace asked.

"When I first approached you, yes, that is always the plan. But as we talked, I don't know, I was so touched by what a wonderful mother you are, what your family means to you, how you worried about your mother and were there for your dad. Even though your husband didn't give you the attention you deserve, you never spoke ill of him, you kept to your promise to be a good wife. Everything you do is for your family and others; you are so unselfish and generous with your time and your love. You are so smart and successful. I love the business world and to hear how you lead your company captured my heart. I've talked to many women in my life and I'd never met anyone like you."

"So, you liked the peek I gave you into my life. Then what, where did you expect it to lead?" Grace replied.

"I prayed to God every day to give me a way to tell you. The thought of losing you even though I was deceiving you, was too much for me. I would rather have a fake relationship with you than risk losing you. I dreamed of being your husband, being there with you, comforting you, telling you every single day how much I appreciate how wonderful you are," I type, my heart feeling full of love for her. I am cautious but hopeful she won't leave.

"So.... do you work alone?" Grace asks.

I pause, I can't tell her about this ugly business. I know I must be honest; she will see through anything less.

"No one works alone in this or any business, Grace," being as vague as I can.

"I figured that. So, do others pretend to be Andrew and write to me too? I really need to know who is on the other end. Again, I want to know your name, you owe me that," Grace is pushing for answers. And if anyone deserves answers, it's her.

"I refused to give anyone your contact information. They know about you, but I kept you for myself," I reply honestly.

"Why? Did you think I was an easy target?"

"No, I wanted to protect you. I wasn't lying when I said I have feelings for you Grace. You have no idea how you have influenced me. I didn't believe in love before you. I only saw opportunity. Then I met you. You were so different. Smart, successful, and you talked intelligently about any subject I could throw at you. You opened my eyes to new ideas; you gave me a new perspective about American women. Yes, groups share their clients with each other, but I didn't share you. They asked me, even begged me. I said no."

"You didn't answer the second part of my question," she persists.

"Yes, you are right, I didn't. Are you coming for me? Are you going to turn me over to the American authorities?"

"I need to go now. I need to cook dinner for my children. You take care, ok? I'm glad we talked," Grace says.

"Grace? One more thing before you go?" I am reaching, grasping for her.

"Yes, what it is?" Grace asks.

"Immanuel. That's my name," I close my eyes, not believing I just told her my real name.

"Thank you. It's nice to finally meet you," Grace replies and is gone.

CHAPTER 36

I am overjoyed. For the first time in my life, I have hope. She talked to me! Me, Immanuel, she talked to me. I'm rushing around my home, cleaning, straightening things, trying to release some of this wonderful energy coursing through my veins. When everything is done to my satisfaction, I take a shower and lay on my bed, trying to slow my heartbeat. I hear the sounds of the night garden outside, and in the distance the sounds of the city. My mind finally at peace, I close my eyes and sleep well for the first time in years.

A few days pass, Grace and I exchange short chats each day. Just friendly check ins with one another, reinforcing to me what a kind soul she is. I ask about her dad and her children and she shares that they are well and a little about what they've been doing. I admit that I don't have a son and have never been married. I tell her that I think thirty is my real age. I tell her that my mother is dead, about my father, and my auntie. She makes me want to be an open book to her. I love hearing from her, about her life and the way that she takes care of everything and everyone.

Getting a little more nerve, I am starting to be more forward with her. Since she started talking to me again, I slip in small expressions of my affection to see if she will react. So far, she hasn't acknowledged my words to her, but that's okay. I know she is still sorting out her feelings for this person she literally knows very little about and what she does know, she isn't sure it's true.

I don't know where this is going or if I can even call her my friend. Or what she would call me. Time will tell. For now, I'm just so happy that she is back. I can tell she has a multitude of questions to ask me. But, in her style, she is proceeding slowly, confirming what she knows and asking minor things that I feel safe answering. I know more is coming though. I trust where we are now in our conversations, but I am cautious. She could easily take me down.

Like every morning, my phone vibrates on the nightstand before I awake. With clients all over various time zones, messages come at all hours.

"Immanuel, may I ask you something?" Grace types.

I smile, so happy that it's her.

"Yes, of course you may, I may not be able to answer though, you know that," I reply.

"Actually, it's more of promise I'd like to make to one another," she says.

"Alright, let's see what you've got for me. And what terms are attached," I say, trying to be lighthearted.

"Our entire relationship from the beginning was based on a lie. I felt connected to you from the very beginning, we had so much in common and could talk for hours. I shared details about my life with you and I never lied to you. I think that even though you lied about who you were, I think much of what you shared is true. Not your career, the story about your friend, or your son. I mean your opinions, views on spirituality, business, and the state of the world. I think that was really you. I want us to promise to one another that we will always be honest. Honest even when it's painful. And if there is something you aren't comfortable telling me yet, just say that. I will respect that boundary and you can respect mine. I fell for you Immanuel; I need to sort out what I believed with who you really are if we are to be friends and understand one another. No more lies, no half-truths, it's all truth from now on. And some of that truth needs to be about your business. I'm not judging, I just want to understand. Will you give me that?" she asks.

"I will give you the world someday, Grace. And yes, I will give you honesty from now on. You are correct, much of what I wrote to you was true. The story about my friend dying, was a setup we use to ask for funds. But I couldn't proceed, I had feelings for you, you were so different from everyone else. I feel ridiculous for trying that stunt on you. I'm sorry. Please understand how difficult it is for me to trust. I don't let people into my life. Ever. It's too risky. I need to be a ghost, if I need to disappear, I just do. I don't know what you did to me Grace. No one ever made me feel the way you do. I wanted to tell you everything, lay my confession at your feet and beg for your mercy. But I didn't, I was a coward. I was too afraid of losing the fragile relationship I did have with you to be a man and tell you my truth," I reply.

"Good, then we have a pact, honesty or silence, nothing in between?" she asks.

"Yes, I agree to that. I would give you my word, but I haven't proven that has much value so far, so I'll just confirm that I agree to be honest or silent," I answer.

"What is it like being a Nigerian?" Grace asks.

"I didn't tell you my country...." I type, completely stunned that she guessed correctly.

"Are you pleading silence on this one? You are from Nigeria, right?" she asks again.

"Yes, I am Nigerian. You scare me Grace. How did you know that?" I feel my hands shaking and I walk to the window to be sure no one is waiting for me in the street as I text back.

"Lucky guess. Don't be scared, I'm not outside with the authorities waiting to pounce," she replies with a laughing emoji.

"I'm not sure if that makes me feel better or not. If not today, when? Will you take me down, Grace?" I ask.

"I think you know me better than that. What do I have to gain by crushing you? Do you think that revenge for a broken heart is my style?" Grace says.

"No, you wouldn't do that. Although I completely believe that you are smart enough to find and punish me. I think your heart is too kind for that though. You would rather understand someone's situation than judge and punish," I say, hoping I'm right.

"You do know me, Immanuel. So, go ahead, what is it like living in Nigeria? What is the situation that made you decide to take this approach to earning a living?" she asks.

I pause, thankful, that she didn't call me a scammer, Yahoo boy or any of the other terms used to describe what I do again. I can't hear those ugly words about me come from her. I want her to respect me; if it takes my entire life, someday I will earn her respect.

"I love my home, but Nigeria is a country that has corruption on every level. Authorities put their own gain above the welfare of the people they were elected or appointed to serve. When the leaders show this behavior, what do you think the people do? Early in our childhood, we learned what bribery was. Did you know, Grace, that when an exam was given, the teachers would often walk to each student's desk, waiting for the student to slip a payment to them? Depending on what the pupil can pay often determined their grade. A child quickly learns to hustle and bargain his way to what he wants or even needs. If he is strong enough, he will simply take what he wants. So, at the same time, he learns to fight. But young people here must fight and hustle, there isn't enough resources available to common people to go around. The resources should be abundant, we have oil and natural resources like no other in Africa. But it is all controlled by foreign interests, our government sells out at the expense of its people at every opportunity. The prices are high, and the wages are low, if you are lucky enough to get a job. When one job comes open, there will be 50, even 100 people apply. And you know who will get that job? Whoever is related to the business owner, knows someone with authority or can pay the bribe. The businesses know they must play the game too. They can make a payment to officials if a building code or other violation is found. Then it's back to business as usual, until they come to collect for their silence again," I explain.

"Nigerian men are expected to provide for their families. I don't just mean their wives and children. Unlike most Americans, we must pay for our younger siblings' and cousins' school fees and other needs and send money to our parents for their expenses. Even aunties, grandparents, uncles, and cousins expect support if you have any income. It is a source of pride for a man to be able to do this. It is expected by all parents and shows that they raised a good son. If a son doesn't do this, after some time, it is like they are dead to their family, a shameful thing. What do you think of that Grace?" I pause, waiting for her response.

I have never talked with anyone about my country, especially a white woman. I think she will be empathetic and interested, but there is no way she can understand how terrible the conditions are here. No way, not someone who has never been hungry for days, been sick but had no doctor or medicine; no way she can truly understand my country. She has never seen anything but wealth.

Grace just politely asks me to continue, not offering sympathy or her thoughts about anything I've said. So, I go on.

"The infrastructure is terrible. The roads that are paved are few, mostly in the wealthiest areas, where most citizens would never be welcome. The power grids are unreliable. We lose power daily in our homes and businesses. The internet signal is often poor too and many areas in the country have no access at all. But jobs, Grace, we need jobs and there are none. It doesn't matter your age, skill level, or if you have a degree, there isn't enough jobs to go around. That's all I can say, the situation here isn't like anything you have ever seen, I'm sure of it," I finish, suddenly tired.

"Immanuel, you are right, I don't know what it's like. But right and wrong doesn't change based on circumstances, no matter how bad. What you have done is stealing and lying, you know that, even if you think it's justified. I'll leave it at that. I'm not your mother, your wife, or anything else. I don't think any less of you as a person, if you hope to change someday, I'll be supportive. If not, that's up to you," Grace says.

"Grace, I'd like to call you every day. Would that be okay?" I ask.

"Really, why?" she asks.

I pause, "Because one of my favorite things about you is your voice. You speak softly, you calm my soul. I always hoped you would save me." I say, hoping for her to agree.

"Ok, sure, I think that would be okay. Just not right now. I need to do some things; I really should go. Before you call, just message me first to be sure I'm free please. Take care, Immanuel."

"Yes, Grace, I will. Be safe, my beauty," I type, but she has already gone.

CHAPTER 37

My spirits are high, and for once, I feel like I have hope. I busy myself cleaning my home, admiring the fine things I have accumulated by my hard work. I go to my bedroom, my sanctuary as I call it. I enter my large walk in closet, brushing by the designer clothes all hanging according to style and color. My shoes are shelved, labeled, and covered to keep them dust free and like new. I don't dress up often, but I need to be prepared when the occasion arises. Grace would like to see me in these fine clothes. I'm sure she appreciates a well-dressed man. At the back of the closet, I open the safe I had built into the wall. I check my belongings here nearly every day. No one knows this is here, but one can't be too careful. Even with a locking gate and security system, I am still very careful. A thief could break in, it happens to people all the time. If your home looks well kept, people assume that there are items of value inside. Hustling, always looking for easy opportunity; that's what thieves do.

I reach inside and pull out my stack of naira, counting slowly, to be sure it's all there. I place it back next to my crypto wallet. Behind that, I keep various prescriptions, in case I need some quick, easy money. Then, a switchblade, an exact match to the one I keep in my bedside table, a Glock 19 and Sig Sauer P365. Satisfied with my check that everything is accounted for and safe, I lock up. Walking back through the closet, I imagine how perfect Grace's dresses and clothes would look here with mine.

I am in a good mood and want to be around people, and decide to drive to the local pub. The game should be on and I can have a drink. I will drink to love and happiness. I pull my car into an open spot near the back of the pub and notice the car that Amobi was driving when he came to my home. I walk over to it, noticing he hasn't licensed it and thinking to myself that he probably never will. I doubt it's even really his. It's older but a nice Mercedes model. The black paint is a bit faded, showing its age, but for Amobi, it's the best thing he has ever owned and may ever will. Maybe five million naira or less. He doesn't have that kind of money, so my suspicion is right. It's stolen. What an idiot.

I walk in the bar and see him right away. He looks surprised to see me. I guess he left me for dead the other day. He sees me walking his direction and waves me over next to him at the bar. He looks like he would rather not see me, but too bad. I need to keep tabs on him. He isn't smart enough to avoid attention and as a result, trouble.

"Wetin dey?" he asks, not making eye contact.

"Nawa oh! U baff up?" I greet him, commenting on his new clothes.

"Yea, man, but look at you. How much this one cost?" he points to my designer jacket.

I laugh, ignoring him.

"Make we go shayo. I'll buy," I tell him, hoping he will relax and tell me where he got funds to get the car or whatever method he took to get it.

"Okay, yes, get me another beer," Amobi says and seems to be less tense next to me now.

I motion for the bartender and he brings our usual. I take a long, slow sip of my whiskey, thinking of Grace. I am so glad she is back; I can't help thinking about a future with her.

"So, what's on your mind? Or should I say who?" Amobi asks.

"Nothing, nobody. Just glad to be out again and enjoy the game," I respond, glancing up to check the score in case he makes a comment and realizes I haven't even looked at the game since getting here.

"Hmmmm, seems like you are thinking about someone. The American?" Amobi says without looking at me.

"Don't worry about her, Amobi. Don't mention her. I don't want you even thinking about her," I glare at him, feeling the blood fill my head and throb.

"No way, man. I've got better things to think about than her, no wahala," he laughs.

"Where's my laptop you were going to return?" I ask. He has pissed me off now. I want to have him watched day and night.

"Actually, it's in the car, let's go get it, since you are finished with your drink. I thought I heard you say you were leaving," he glares back, challenging me.

"Yeah, I think I am going now. I forgot I don't really care for the clientele who come here," I say, rising to leave.

We walk to his car in silence, Amobi leading the way. He is a bit taller than me but thinner. He doesn't take care of himself in business or his physical health. He looks older than his twenty-seven years in my opinion. When you are always scheming and having to watch your back, one tends to let one's head hang, in a shameful way. He is slightly slouched, and walks like he wants to find a shadow to hide in. He doesn't want to be in the sunlight for long, someone will see him for what he truly is. Amobi unlocks the boot of the car and I see my laptop scattered in parts.

"Well, there it is. You said you can fix it," he says, like it's just a matter of clicking a piece back together.

I grab it and look it over.

"You've removed the hard drive," I look at his face, "I want it back."

"I don't think I have it anymore. I couldn't find it anyway," he says, still not looking at me.

"We will go to your house and find it. I'll follow you," I turn and walk to my car, not giving him time to say no.

In my car, I see a message from Grace, wishing me sweet dreams.

I message her back and she comes online.

"Can I call you? I'm driving and only have a minute, but I want to ask you something", I write, and she quickly replies yes.

I dial her and we exchange small talk. God, I love the sound of her voice....

"Grace, are you okay? Financially, I mean?" I ask.

"Yes, I'm fine, why?" she asks.

"I just want to be sure. I never want anything to happen that would make you worry about money, baby. I'll send you what you need, you know that, right?"

"I'm fine, Immanuel, I swear. I had an issue at the same time my husband left, but it's all taken care of now, so don't worry," she says and my stomach falls.

"What do you mean? What happened?" I ask.

"Someone hacked an account. But the bank restored almost all my funds. Fortunately, I could prove I didn't authorize the transactions," she explained.

"You said transactions, plural. There were multiple? How much was taken?" I ask, already knowing the answer.

"About $14,000 over a period of a few months, Immanuel. Why are you asking? It happens. The bank said it wasn't any mistake I had made or anyone I knew, just the usual cyber stuff," Grace's voice is starting to sound nervous.

"I just read an article about how often that happens, and I want to be sure you are taking precautions and are safe. The article said women are often easy targets. You said your bank restored the money to you? All of it?" I ask, trying to keep my voice calm. I can hear my blood pulsing in my ears as I stare at Amobi's car about two lengths ahead, turning onto his street.

"Yes, minus a liability limits and fees. I assure you, I'm fine, Immanuel. I have all the security features on my accounts and computers. I'm confident it won't happen again. I am watching much closer than I used to, and I've had an education about how scamming works now. I may know more than you, Immanuel," she says laughing.

"Maybe, my angel, maybe so. You are very intelligent. We will talk more later, there's something I need to do right now. I love you, Grace," the words are out of my mouth before I realize that's the first time, I've said that to her as Immanuel. I pause and go for broke.

"I mean it, Grace, I love you. You mean everything to me."

"I uh, it's just, well I don't know what to say to that, Immanuel. Be safe, okay. We will talk soon," Grace says.

"Yes, and I'm here for you, whatever you need. I'll talk to you later," I hang up and stop the car behind Amobi on the street in front of his house. His home is modest but nicer than most in Nigeria. It could be much nicer if he would take pride in it. Trash was scattered in the front garden, either blown there by the wind or he tossed it down. Either way, he paid no attention to it and we stepped around bottles and debris in the path.

We enter his home through a side door, he doesn't glance back to see if I lock it behind us or even pull it shut. I pull it shut, letting my eyes adjust to the low light.

"The power is dim again. No help for that. It won't help to look for the hard drive when you don't have light, my man," he says, flopping onto a couch, obviously not intending to help me look at all.

125

"I'll be fine, Amobi. Be sure you get some rest there while I look," I say, thinking what a disgusting human being he is. I see a small desk in the corner of the main room. I really only remember being here the day he moved in; I haven't been invited back since. Typical of our friendship, I'm only a friend if I have something he wants.

I see the hard drive lying on the desk next to the new laptop he took from me. It's on top of an external drive which is plugged into the laptop, so I know he has already copied any files I didn't remove.

"Why don't you clean up your place? Show some respect. You don't even offer me a seat or something to drink?" I ask, hating him more each minute.

"Why should I do that? You enter my home and prowl around like I'm different than you? Like you aren't a thief like the rest of us? Or can you not admit that to yourself? Your American wouldn't like that, would she?" Amobi spews at me.

"Shut your fucking mouth! Don't you dare say anything about her. Or about me. You are disgusting and you always will be," I am trying to control my voice and keep from lunging at him.

"Oh, I have lots to say about the American. Next time you talk to her, whispering your sweet nothings, saying all the things she wants to hear to get you what you want, tell her I said thank you," he smiles at me like a deranged cat, ready to pounce.

"What the hell are you saying? You did not talk to her! You stay away from her, I'll kill you if you contact her," I am shouting at him.

"I don't have to talk to her. She already paid off. She bought me a car, new clothes, a whore I met in the club; your precious American paid for me to have a very good time. And I didn't have to say one word to her, you did all the hard work for me. The links were easy to find, Immanuel, I told you this woman is making you soft," he smiles, and leans back on the couch, closing his eyes, looking quite satisfied with himself.

He's right, I am getting soft. I sent Grace the links early on before I knew I loved her. I should have removed the potential damage, but I didn't protect her. I was too involved in my feelings to remember to keep her safe. I am filled with hatred for Amobi and even more hatred for myself. It's more than I can take. I am on top of him in seconds, my hands around his throat, screaming at him. His eyes are bulged, and he is gasping for air, but I am not letting go. I said I'll kill him, and I will. He twists his skinny body and brings his knee up into my crotch very hard. It knocks the wind out of me, I release my grip and step back to try to catch my breath. He lunges at me and I dodge him.

"She's a wealthy whore, Immanuel. There's more than enough there for both of us. You can have her, if that's all you want, but I'm telling you, she won't miss the funds," Amobi's eyes are wide, I can see the fear in them.

I step forward and grab him by the shirt that my Grace's money purchased. The feel of fine silk against my hands makes me more furious. He is an animal and doesn't deserve to breathe. I draw my fist back and hit him hard in the stomach, forcing him to bend forward. My fist cuts upward, finding his stupid face, I can feel blood covering my hand, but nothing can make me stop. I want to keep beating him until he is dead.

"Immanuel! Amobi! What the hell! Let him go, you are killing him!" Enofi runs into the door and grabs me around the waist. I knew I should have locked that door. I sling Enofi off my back and take one more punch at the scum's stupid face. I feel his jaw break and I pull back and let him slump to the floor.

"What is hell happened, Immanuel? God damn, he needs to go the hospital," Enofi is shouting, not able to comprehend what is going on.

"Then take him. He's your problem, not mine. If he ever crosses my path again, he will wish he died today," I say, grabbing the hard drive, computer and all the components I can find. I take his phone just to be sure. I step over Amobi's body and push past Enofi on my way out.

"You will not say who did this to him if you know what is good for you. You be sure you keep him quiet after they unwire his jaw," I glare at him, backing out through the door.

CHAPTER 38

Outside, I check the street, making sure there is no one out as I make my way to my car. I drop everything in the back of the car and walk back to Amobi's front garden. I wash my hands at the faucet, scrubbing his disgusting blood from my skin. The adrenaline has me shaking and wishing Enofi hadn't interrupted and I could have killed him.

I splash water onto my face and hair and walk to the window to see my reflection. There is no blood on my face, I don't think he even got a punch in at me. I see some young boys up the street playing stickball, but they don't even look my way. In Nigeria, people know not to get involved. If anyone heard the shouting and fight from Amobi's house, they aren't even looking this direction. There is enough trouble here, no one wants to borrow any more.

I ease behind the wheel of my car, willing my pulse to slow a bit before pulling away. I see Enofi dragging Amobi out to his car. Amobi is walking a bit but leaning hard on his friend, still very disoriented. He will live, but he is dead to me. I just hope I got all connection to Grace removed from his house. I wait up the street until I see Enofi's car leave the block. I quickly pull my car back into the drive and enter Amobi's house again. I can't leave anything to chance.

I take my time, searching through drawers, cabinets, under the bed, leaving nothing uncovered. I find some naira in a shoebox and take it without counting it. This is will be returned to Grace and I will make up any difference this piece of shit took from her. I find some jewelry and some guns and take those as well. It's the price he must pay. After an hour, I decide I have looked everywhere a simple-minded thug like Amobi would think to hide something, I shut out the lights and lock the door behind me. If it is left unlocked, he will have squatters here within a day's time. As much as I hate him, he doesn't deserve to come home to that.

The sun is starting to set, and I glance at the clock in my car as I cruise away from Amobi's neighborhood. It's 830pm, I have an overwhelming need to call Grace, knowing that I will wake her. But I must hear her voice.

The phone rings three times before she answers with a sleepy hello.

"Immanuel, what's wrong? It's 230 in the morning," she says softly.

"I know, baby. I'm so sorry, I had to call. I took care of some things tonight to ensure that you are safe and can trust me. There's one more thing I need to do, and it can't wait," I say.

"What is it, Immanuel? What happened?" she asks.

"Will you turn on your video? I want you to see my face. I want you to know who I am," I say, my heart hoping she will say yes.

"Ok, but I am a mess. You woke me, you know," she says, switching to video as I do the same.

"Grace, can you see me? You look so beautiful. Oh my god, I never imagined how beautiful you look in the night," I say. "What do you think? Am I worse than you imagined?"

"No, Immanuel, you are a very handsome man. Very handsome, your skin is beautiful," Grace smiles at me through the phone. She smiled at me! Me! Not some persona, not some military officer.

"Grace, you have made my dreams come true. I can't tell you how many nights I wanted to show you who I am," I can't quit looking at her. I pull into my gate and up the drive.

"Are you just getting home? I see your home and lawn behind you, it's lovely," Grace says.

"Yes, this is my home. Come inside with me, I'll show you around," I offer.

"I'd like that. Immanuel, thank you for finally showing me who you are. It means so much to me," Grace says softly.

I enter my home and drop my keys on the table by the door, my heart is full. I want to tell her everything, but I know everyone would tell me to be cautious. I show her around my house, all the rooms, the garden, even the bathrooms and my closet. I want her to be part of my world. This feels perfect, being at home with her.

"Grace, earlier you said your husband had left. Tell me what happened."

"Oh, yes. Well, basically, my worst suspicions were true. He is having an affair with his secretary. So now I know why he never came to bed or seemed to have time for me. We are still married, but he moved out."

"Grace, I'm so sorry. He is an idiot to have done this to you. How are the children?"

"They are okay, honestly, they've adjusted very well. He wasn't just distant to me, you know. He never seemed to have time for them either. He provided for them in every way but was always too busy to spend much time with any of us. The girls said he was always in a bad mood when he was home anyway, and they felt like they had to walk on eggshells around him."

"Walk on eggshells? What does that mean?"

"Oh sorry, it means, they had to be careful not to upset him. What would you say to describe that in Nigeria?" Grace says, laughing.

"Oh, maybe people say that here, I don't know. I just say tread carefully, I guess but walking on eggshells describes it very well. So, what does the future hold, Grace?"

"I don't know yet. I have lawyer and have discussed the various scenarios, but I haven't filed for divorce. We aren't legally separated either, he just moved out. He is still paying half the bills and seeing the kids when the schedule works for all of us to get together. But I have nothing to say to him. Honestly, I don't even miss him. I guess emotionally he left so long ago that I didn't really have a husband anyway. And I agree with the girls, when he was home, I felt like I was walking on eggshells. He wasn't ever violent; I don't want you to think that. We never even fought, it was like we were business partners or roommates rather than married."

"I'm very sorry Grace. I had never been married so I don't know if I would be any help at all, but I'm here if you need to talk."

"Thank you, Immanuel. You know, over the last year, I don't feel like you and I have ever run out of things to talk about. Even when I discovered you had deceived me and we weren't talking, things would happen during the day or I would read something and I'd think, I need to tell Andrew about this....and then I would remember and pain was there just as real as the first time. I missed you then. I loved you so much but more than that, you were my closest friend since I have been an adult. After college, I was so focused on trying to perfect everything in my life, that I forgot to keep in touch with old friends or even try to make new ones. The children, the house, work, my husband's business, took all my time. I didn't even have time to stop and think about what I wanted or needed in life, I only had time to finish one thing and start the next. I think most Americans are that way. We are terrible at vacations, all of us check email and take phone calls anyway, like we never left the office. Even when my mother died, I worried about missing important issues at work. But you know if I quit, there will be someone else in my job within weeks and it would be like I was never there. That's really sad when you think about it. In a country with enormous wealth compared to much of the world, we are poor emotionally. So many people are lonely here."

"I'm sorry it is that way. You deserve better. Your children love you; you deserve to enjoy them and be taken care of like a queen. That's what you are, you know? You have built a kingdom by yourself. Yes, I know your husband was part of it, but without you, it's nothing. I love the woman you are Grace. I will love you in this life and the next. I don't even have to promise you that, there's nothing I can do to stop it, I am meant to love you, even if we never meet, I am connected to you."

"What do you plan to do with your life, Immanuel?"

"I want to build a life. A good life. I want children. I want to provide for them. I want to travel, to read, to learn, have good food, fresh air, and beauty around me. I want to be a better man than I am today. I want to see you, know you, and protect you. At the end, if I do that, I will die happy."

"I think that's the best answer to that question I have ever heard."

"You make me want to be better than I am, Grace. I am human and in a bad situation but.... only I can change that. I hope you will see me through."

"Immanuel, I need to go wake the children for school and get ready for work. Look at me before I go, ok?"

I look deep into her eyes, wishing my phone's screen was larger or better yet, she was standing in front of me and I could reach out to her.

"I love you Immanuel. I don't know what this is or why the universe brought us together, but I love you."

"I love you, Grace. You've made me the happiest man in the world."

She smiles and waves goodbye before the screen goes dark. I sit staring at the blank screen for a long time after we hang up. I can't believe this; how could I be so blessed?

CHAPTER 39

Later in the week, I see Enofi in the market. He seems glad to see me and approaches me with more respect than in the past. After we exchange greetings, I ask him about Amobi. He tells me that he is out of the hospital, but his jaw will stay wired shut for a few months. He was angry when he saw that I had gone through everything in his house, but he knew that I would. He told Enofi that I got everything he had that could give him access to "the American" and was disappointed that he would no longer be able to provide for himself through her accounts.

"Listen Immanuel, my brother...you know I always call you my brother, right?" Enofi begins.

"Yeah, sure I know," I reply, waiting for him to make his point.

"You know, Amobi and I weren't ever really that good of friends or business partners. I was always watching my back around him. I told him I think he deserved the beating you gave him, and he should be thankful you spared his life."

"I would have killed him if you hadn't stopped me. I am glad you arrived when you did, Enofi. I don't need to be convicted for killing him. I have better things to do than sit in a prison, especially for someone who doesn't deserve to live anyway."

"You really do love the American... she isn't another client to you Immanuel? You don't just see her as your ticket out of this place? Sometimes opportunity and love look very similar, my brother. I would have never guessed in a lifetime you would fall in love. You taught me this game and that is the first rule, leave your heart out of it. Maybe Almighty God Chukwu has smiled on you and will give you children with her, I don't know. Just be careful man, she could be your death," Enofi smiles and seems somewhat happy for me.

"I know man, but this is real. Thanks, I'll be careful. I know what I'm doing, don't worry. I'll see you around," I walk away from him as my phone buzzes in my pocket.

Within an hour of that call, I find myself exiting an Aston Martin that picked me up from the market. I have been asked to meet a business associate at his home on the other side of Lagos to discuss some business that needs to be done in Canada within the next month. The chauffer opens the door for me, and I step out in front of one of the biggest homes on this part of the island. I am inwardly thankful that I always make it a priority to dress my best when I am out in public, even when going to the market area. Even if I don't encounter my business partners, I get respect from the vendors and locals when I dress well. That's something most of the younger Yahoo boys will never understand. One must dress well but not draw unneeded attention.

The important associate meets with me for only a few minutes but is welcoming and offers me a whiskey. I accept the drink and compliment his home and family, praising him for being a successful and important man.

The request is to travel to Montreal and make a delivery to some important associates there. I must be discreet, as always, and not tell anyone my real name but they will know who has sent me. All travel arrangements will be made on my behalf, the packages will be available for me before I leave. I have no questions for my associate and know better than to ask any. He grows silent and I know that is my cue to leave. I thank my host for his hospitality and offer thanks to his three wives standing at the door as I return to the waiting car.

I have done similar work for others, but this man is operating on a higher level than most. I commit do the job well so I am in his favor as there could be a profitable future for me with him. I'm excited for the opportunity but have much work to do to prepare to leave Nigeria.

CHAPTER 40

Later at home, I organize my travel documents, although I will be given false documents for this job. I just want to be prepared and cause no delay to my associate. I have never been to Montreal, but I'm sure it's cold since it is now autumn. I will need to buy a coat and some appropriate clothes. After I've gone through my legitimate travel documents, I decide to go shopping.

I know the one place to go for a businessman's upscale wardrobe. I drive to Victoria Island to browse their designer showrooms. I'll be in Canada for a week, so my purchase will include at least three suits, dress shirts, dress pants, two pair of designer shoes and a belt. I am lucky enough to find a long black wool trench coat and a fedora. The ladies working at the stores told me they have many customers who travel internationally so they always keep coats and winter clothes in stock. After I pay for my purchases and I'm walking toward the door, a royal blue evening gown by Halston captures my attention. Wow, that would look perfect on Grace! The dress would hug her curves perfectly and has a slit up the left leg. The bodice has delicate beading over the silk fabric and the neckline comes up to the mannikin's collarbones. But the back drapes open plunging down to the waistline. I must buy it for her. I asked one of the ladies for assistance as I describe Grace's body shape to determine what size to buy. The store owner was about Grace's size and offered to try it on so I could see how the fabric moved.

I waited somewhat patiently outside the dressing area while she changed. When she emerged into the store, I knew it was perfect. The fabric moved flawlessly. I couldn't take my eyes off her, but I was only seeing Grace. I immediately said I'll take it, wrap it up immediately for me please.

All the women smiled at one another, picking up on the fact that I hadn't even asked the price. I didn't care, I wanted to see Grace in that dress and escort her on my arm more than anything in the world. I would have paid any price for that.

I secured my purchases in my car and pulled out to fight the traffic. The street sounds were deafening. Cars honking to no avail, scooters and bikes weaving in and out of traffic, people crossing the street regardless of the oncoming traffic. If the traffic were moving fast enough, they could be injured, but there's no chance of that. Everywhere, too many people, and not enough roads or vehicles. People were hanging out of small trucks and packed into vans. Some were even on the outside of the vehicle moving along the road. Who knows if they knew the driver or they just jumped on to get a free ride.

After about an hour on the sweltering street, I ease my car into the parking lot of a national bank. At this bank, I have an account in which I hold funds for Amobi, Enofi and I. I need to make a withdrawal, so I have some of my own cash for my trip. I never granted Amobi access to the account, but I did include Enofi's name just in case somethings ever happens to me. He isn't always of the same mindset as I am, but he is reasonable enough to take care of things and stay discreet.

I walk through the tall glass doors into the air-conditioned grand entrance of the bank. And to think people would call me a thief! Banks are the biggest criminal organizations on earth. Their sole purpose is to keep one in debt so they can hold onto a person's money and invest it for themselves. Everyone working here is well dressed and attractive. Like they want their customers to believe their money is in beautiful hands, so that makes it safe.

Greeting the young woman at one of the clerk's desk, I ask to see my account balance and make a withdrawal. She politely asks my name and within seconds provides me with my balance.

"What did you say?" I lean forward and quietly ask.

She repeats the amount and I sit back, stunned. "Are you sure that is my account?"

She repeats my name and address back to me. "Is there a problem?"

"Yes, that is me, I just, well, I guess I hadn't checked on the balance for some time as I have accounts at other banks, and I didn't remember how much I had saved. And, of course, with your fine institution's interest rate at such a generous level, one can't help but be successful," I offer my compliments to cover my shock.

"Of course, we do intend to be competitive for the business of successful men like yourself," she smiles, ever the loyal employee.

I fill out my form for the withdrawal and am promptly presented with an envelope of funds. She asks if there is anything else, she can do for me. I decline and wish her a good day.

I am shaking as I walk to my car, there is an extra 16 million naira in the account. How can this be? As soon as I am inside my car, I lock the doors and just sit staring ahead. After allowing my heart to slow enough that I can't hear it beating in my ears, I open my banking app on my phone. I hate any banking on my phone, but I don't have my laptop with me. It's always such a risk here to do business on a phone and especially using open Wi-Fi.

I scroll through the transactions. Small amounts, no more than 6 million naira at a time coming in from various places in the UK, then some from Greece, South America, and the Philippines. What is this? They are all small but spaced only days apart. Only once is there two listed in a day, but those are from South America and the Philippines so it may have been due to the time difference. Could Amobi be involved in this? His name isn't on the account though, only Enofi....

My flight leaves at noon tomorrow for Montreal and I still need to double check that I have everything prepared. My employer's men will pick me up in the morning and will have all the paperwork and instructions for me. But before that, I need to speak with Enofi.

He has made big returns in the past but has always discussed them with me in anticipation of the windfall. Even though individually these deposits aren't large, they must somehow be connected. I sit in the parking lot of the bank, listening to the phone ring, waiting for Enofi.

"Yeah, Immanuel, what is going on? I'm in the middle of something, so keep this short, okay?" Enofi sounds like he is out of breath.

"Are you with a woman? You sound like you can't catch your breath," I ask, annoyed, and wanting to get to the point.

"Yeah. But keep it quiet, man. You know I'm not supposed to be seeing her anymore. Swear to me, okay?" he says.

Now I remember, he has been sleeping with Amobi's sister. Amobi threatened to kill him over it because she is married, but Enofi doesn't seem to mind that.

"Whatever, man, do what you want on that. I want to ask you about all the deposits in our main account lately. What is going on?"

"Oh, I set up some pulls, that's all," he says, still breathless.

"Where from? They appear to be from all over. I know you aren't talking to that many people," I keep probing.

"Yeah, the money was routed around a bit before it landed in our account. It's mostly from US clients like your Grace," he says offhandedly.

My heart sinks at the sound of her name coming out of his mouth. "What do you mean? You've been pulling from her too?"

"Amobi just had one account of hers. I have some others. Don't worry, she won't miss it, I can assure you of that. It isn't just her money, Immanuel, other clients are being unconsciously generous too. Why are you so soft now? You used to be the best; you never worried about your client. Now that's all you think about. Like they don't have plenty to help out those of us in need? Come on, man, wake up."

I slam down the phone, breathing heavily. Grace is going to think I did this. I have only wanted to protect her. There's no way I can do that now, her information is in the hands of multiple people, not just those two idiots.

I take a couple of breaths and stride back into the bank. I am again welcomed by the well-dressed employees and I ask to speak with a representative privately. At once, I am ushered into an office overlooking the street and a young man enters.

"How may I help you today sir? The staff said you would like to speak privately," he asks, smiling as he seats himself behind the large desk.

"Yes, I have just learned that my company is sending me abroad and it isn't clear when I will be returning to work in Nigeria. I was here earlier today and withdrew some funds for my trip but now it seems my time away will be much longer than originally thought," I explain.

"Yes, very good. We wish you much success while you are away and look forward to your business when you return, of course. I'm sorry, sir, I didn't get your name?" the young banker asks.

I share my name and account information as he verifies everything on the computer to the side of him, positioned so he can still maintain eye contact and personal service to his customer.

"Ok, yes, here we are. Now, how can I assist? I see you did take a withdrawal earlier today, like you said. Do you wish to withdraw more since your plans have been changed?"

"Yes, I think so. Is it possible for me to close the account? I do have another business associate on the account, but he will actually be going with me, so it might be best to just close it until we return," I explain.

"I'm sorry, we are unable to close it without his consent and signature, but we could freeze it for you. After you make your withdrawal, of course. No other deposits or withdrawals will be accepted. You just need to leave a small amount in the account to keep it open. Then, when you return, just come into the bank and it's only a matter of your signature to unfreeze it. Since you are requesting just a hold placed on the account, your business associate doesn't need to be with you. However, if he comes to the bank without you, we will need to contact you to open it again."

"That's exactly what I had in mind. Could you provide me with a withdrawal document? I'll try not to take any more of your time, you have been most kind," I say, completing the form to withdraw all but a very small sum.

The young banker excused himself to access the cash drawer and quickly returned with my funds. He asked me to count it in front of him to be sure I am satisfied. I count 16 million naira and then count it again to be sure. I offer him my sincerest thanks and exit his office.

The evening traffic has eased up, most people were home by now, eating their dinner and talking with their spouses and children about their day. I never desired that life. The ordinary routine, the same people in your home day after day. The same woman in your bed every night. But now, that peacefulness, that consistency appeals to me. I have everything else, but I am alone. No one greets me when I enter my gate. No children shouting over one another for my attention. No soft, curvy body to reach out for in the night. I want that. I want to be that man and that father. I know that's what the hole in my heart has needed.

The phone rings through the Bluetooth speakers in my car. I glance at it, irate to see it's Amobi. I answer, beginning to fume at the thought of his voice.

"Man, I wan make you come my house. E get something wey I wan tell you," Amobi says, although it's hard to understand him with his jaw wired. It sounds like someone talking low through a clenched jaw.

"I don't want to see you or hear your stupid voice, Amobi, I told you, you are dead to me. You know what you did, I don't want to hear anymore," I reach for the device to hang up, but he stops me.

"It wasn't me, man. Yes, I took the money when it was given to me and I laughed when I learned where it was from. But I didn't pull it, Enofi pulled it and he still is."

I drive silently, staring ahead, the memory of Enofi in the market swearing he was my brother and how he didn't blame me and would have killed Amobi for what he had done.

"Are you there? I swear, my brother, he came to me with the money that I used to buy my car and party with that woman, but I didn't take it directly from the American. He set it all up and he said there's more where that came from. I thought you should know. I don't care that you have feelings for this woman, but you need to know it wasn't me. And you know he has sold her information to anyone willing to buy. He will continue to make funds off her for a long time. I don't think you can protect her at this point," Amobi says.

"Ok, thanks Amobi. I'll think of something..." I hang up, completely defeated.

CHAPTER 41

I pull through my gate, thankful the light at the side entrance was on. The lights go out so frequently here and I hate walking into a dark house.

Inside, I drop my keys on the small table in the entryway. I take my purchases from my earlier shopping up to my bedroom and lay them on the bed for now. I pull the envelopes from the bank out and secure the money in smaller separate amounts into my bags I've already packed for my trip. I'll keep the coat out and carry it onto the plane. I will look strange with a coat in Lagos, but I'll be thankful for it when I land in Montreal tomorrow. I place the rest of my new business clothes and Grace's dress carefully into my hanging designer suitcase. I will have two bags for the airline to check and my laptop bag for my carryon. Within my laptop bag, I leave plenty of room for the documents my employer will provide me tomorrow.

I sit on the bed, feeling exhausted and hungry. I don't know if I have much to eat in my kitchen but before I go to search, I want to call Grace. I have no idea what to say to her or if she even knows that she has money missing from her accounts. I just want to hear her voice.

I call her through the app so we can video chat. To my surprise, she answers quickly. It must be 2 am there, and, where is she?

"Hello Immanuel, your timing is perfect, I just landed," she says with a smile spread across her beautiful face.

"You just landed? Where are you? I didn't know you were going anywhere," I stammer, completely shocked.

"I'm sorry, I thought I told you. I am speaking at a conference this week in Montreal. I'll be here for three days and then a I took a few extra days to do some sightseeing. I haven't been here since I was a kid. It's such a beautiful city, the museums are incredible. Although October isn't the best time to come. It's snowing already! But as you know, I'm used to the cold," she laughs.

My mind is racing. I can't believe my luck that I can meet her there! I can't tell her what I am doing in Montreal though. I don't think she would believe the coincidence that I am going there on business at the same time as her. I'll just offhandedly ask if I can come to visit her since she will have some free time after her conference. I see her walking through the airport as she is chatting. My window of opportunity is closing quickly. If she gets to the luggage pick up area, she will have to go.

I interrupt her. "Grace, you know, it just occurred to me. I have some free time this week and it sounds like you will too. Would you be opposed if I traveled to Montreal so we could finally meet in person?"

Grace stops walking, and then apologizes to the crowds of people behind her. She is excusing herself to get out of the flow of people rushing to their destinations so we can talk. I wait, smiling at her politeness. Any other person would have just barged through, but not Grace, she is weaving and sidestepping to reach a quiet place. Finally, she makes it to a window.

"Are you serious? You will come to Montreal? This week?"

"Yes, but only if you would allow me to. I don't want to impede into your life or make you feel uncomfortable. When you said you would have a few days, I thought, why not? What is holding me here? Where are you staying?"

"Immanuel, I hope you are serious. I would love to see you; you have no idea how much I would love to finally meet you. I am staying at the Omni Mont Royal."

"Then I will meet you in Montreal. I will see what I can find nearby. I will message you when I arrive, and you can let me know when you will be finished with your conference. Give me about a day to get there and we can connect. I'll let you go so you can get your luggage. I love you Grace. We will be together soon," I smile at her sweet face looking back at me.

"I can't believe this is happening. Yes, we will meet soon, Immanuel. Be safe, I love you too," Grace smiles and does a little wave at me on the screen.

I wink back and blow a kiss. With that, she is gone but soon to be in my arms. She didn't seem upset or distracted so I am guessing she doesn't know that she is missing money once again. I am going to tell her everything and give her back everything that was taken and more. I hope she will forgive me and understand it wasn't me. But I can't stop smiling that I will see her soon.

CHAPTER 42

The next morning, I rush around my home, securing everything and checking again that I have all my personal belongings that I will need in Montreal. I contact a security service that I have used before and book their services to patrol and walk my property three times a day for the next week. My phone rings alerting that the car has arrived to transport me to the airport.

I am greeted by the driver as he opens the back door of the same car that picked me up at the market. Sitting in the back seat waiting for me, is my employer.

"Good morning Immanuel. Did you sleep well?" he greets me.

"Good morning, yes, thank you. You look healthy and well this fine morning," I return his polite greeting as he quickly opens the portfolio in his lap and starts our business.

The car speeds into the morning traffic toward the airport. We will arrive well before my time to check in, but my employer leaves nothing to chance. Missed flights or any other delays in his business are not acceptable, of that I am certain.

He reviews the documents I am to use for boarding and when I check in at the Ritz Carlton in Montreal. A car will be waiting for me at the airport, the driver will be at the luggage area and will remain on retainer for my entire trip. I am allowed a few days to rest after my flight before I meet the business partners to hand off the documents that are to be delivered. That will give me a little bit of time with Grace before I conduct any business. Like my employer, I believe one should be well rested and calm before meeting with any associates. It is rude to appear that one has rushed into a meeting without preparation; one must always appear well rested and confident.

The driver is swift through the morning traffic. He seems to know just when there is a break in between cars and slips into every opportunity to advance his important employer to his destination. We are soon at my gate drop off. My employer wishes me well and gives last minute instructions if I have any difficulty. I am not under any circumstances to contact him while I am abroad. He hands me a business card for a Nigerian businessman in Montreal. Again, I mustn't contact him unless my situation is dire. He instructs me to report for a meeting upon my return, not allowing me any days to rest after my return flight. I thank him for his kindness and assure him that all will be done to his exact specifications.

With that, I am left three hours before my flight on the sidewalk in front of the doors to my gate with my two suitcases and my laptop bag over my shoulder. I am nervous but encounter no issues getting through security and check in. I've brought a book to read so the time I must wait before boarding passes quickly.

I awake to the afternoon sun as the pilot announces our descent into Montreal. The flight announcements have been in both English and French. At least I assume it's French, I don't speak it so I could be proven otherwise. I hope that isn't too much of a barrier for me during my time in Montreal, but I think most Canadians speak English as well. If I remember correctly, Grace told me once that she speaks a little bit, so I will have to rely on her to translate.

I rub my eyes, thankful to be flying business class and to have had a seatmate that kept to himself. The worst thing about flying is sitting with a person who wants to chatter the entire flight. I always bring a book and ear buds to send a clear signal that I do not want to be bothered.

Once we touch down and start taxiing to our gate, the pilot welcomes us to Montreal, temperature is 40 degrees, with sun now, soon turning to rain. I'm thankful I bought a winter coat. I shuffle along through the airport with the masses of people scurrying to get to their luggage or their next departure gate. I finally reach the luggage area and see a young man dressed in business attire and a black coat standing with my luggage. He sees me approach and bids me good morning.

"Pardon me for taking the liberty of securing your bags, sir. My name is Pierre. How was your flight?" he asks.

"Thank you, everything was fine. I appreciate you meeting me here, Pierre," I reply.

"My pleasure. I have taken care of all your arrangements and will remain at your service whenever you need me for your entire stay. You will be staying at the Ritz-Carlton downtown. I trust you will find their service to your liking," he says, handing me his card.

"May I ask, is that near the Omni Mont-Royal?"

"Yes, just a few blocks away. Are you not satisfied with the Ritz, sir? I am happy to make other arrangements," he looks worried.

"No, that won't be necessary at all. My sister once stayed at the Omni, that's why I asked. I recall she said it was near the fine art museum. I hope to have time to tour the area a bit," I answer.

"Yes, sir. I will personally ensure that you have time to see that and anything you would like. You have today and tomorrow completely free of appointments. You might like to rest a bit and then I am happy to coordinate anything you like. Follow me this way, I have the car waiting," he smiles and carries my bags toward the exit.

At the Ritz, Pierre hands me off at the check in desk, again, assuring me that he is only a phone call away, day or night. I am escorted to my room by the attentive staff. My suite is top end, everything is perfectly arranged and welcoming. I unpack, hanging my clothes and Grace's dress in the large closet. I hope that Grace will come here with me. She deserves to stay in a room like this.

CHAPTER 43

I know I should rest, but there's no way, not yet. I am going to walk up the street to the Omni. I won't call Grace yet, I do need to rest before I see her, but I want to familiarize myself with her hotel and the area. Luckily, the sun is still shining, but a cold wind is moving in. I flip the collar of my coat up to shield my ears. Our hotels are separated by a few blocks, just like Pierre said. I enter the Omni and stroll through the lobby area. I follow the signs to the conference room areas. The pharmacy conference is in session. A friendly young lady is at a desk. I smile at her and pick up the itinerary and list of speakers. I briskly walk away as I know she is going to ask for my name and registration information. As I suspected, she doesn't pursue me.

Further ahead is a table of name tags of attendees that are yet to arrive or possibly no shows. Glancing at the table, I pick up a tag that says "Hello, my name is Philip Vellore". I place it in my pocket and slip into an open conference room where a session is already in progress. I find a seat along the perimeter of the room and nod at the man sitting 2 seats down who glances up as I take my seat.

I feign interest in the speaker's topic. He is sharing something about a new chemotherapy drug and the audience seems to be impressed with his graphs and the overall success of this advancement in cancer care. I couldn't care less, trying to nonchalantly scan the room for Grace but I don't see her anywhere. I change my focus to the conference program I took from the desk. On the front cover, she is listed along with the other speakers. A small professional head shot is included next to a short biography. I run my finger along the program through the rest of the day's schedule. On the next page, I find her. She is speaking at 9 am tomorrow.

The same man in my row looks up at me as I rise to leave. I nod a farewell to him. He looks puzzled that I would leave during a presentation but there is only one session at which I want to be present. I leave the conference area and lobby and head back to the Ritz for some relaxation. I'll message Grace late tonight, too late to see her today, but we can make plans for tomorrow. I find myself holding my breath as I think about meeting her. Finally, after so much time, I will finally see her.

The sun has disappeared and now a cold rain has begun. The wool overcoat has already proven to be worth the money. I pull the collar around my neck to keep the rain off. I'll never understand how people live somewhere this cold.

The luxurious bathroom has both a steam shower and a soaking tub. Tonight, I opt for the shower, letting the warmth penetrate my weary skin. It has been a long day, but I still have work to do. After toweling off, I seat myself at the large desk in the office area of the suite. I open the documents and paperwork provided to me to make this delivery. All the instructions are typewritten for me. I am to destroy the passport and ID I used on my trip here to Montreal. Another set has been provided for my return along with a new cell phone. My return flight tickets are loaded onto the airline app on the new phone. The same name is there as the new ID and passport. Among the items are a wedding ring and a pair of glasses for me to resemble the man in the ID and passport photos. There is an envelope of five thousand Canadian dollars with a note that indicates it's for food and miscellaneous expenses.

Finally, I come to the documents to be delivered. They are sealed and I am certain I am not to open them. The printed labels on the front of each has the name of the recipient and a photo of the person is paperclipped to the front. There are four total; three men and one woman. I glance at the itinerary on the new cell phone's calendar and see that I have 2 separate meetings scheduled 2 and then 3 days from now. The names on each of the calendar entries match the names on the packet. The calendar entries give me a short script of what I am to say and exactly how long to spend at each of the two meetings. At the meeting with the man and woman, I will be given a packet to return to my employer. But for the first meeting, I will only be delivering.

Satisfied now that I am organized and know as much of the plan as needed, I open my laptop to do some of my own work. I log onto the various chat rooms to check in on my current clients. I have messages from all of them as usual. I start with the clients in the UK as they will be sleeping now so I can message, and it will be waiting for them when they awake. Finishing those, I start with the US and quickly engage in conversation with a woman from Arizona. She isn't one of my favorites, but she divorced a corporate businessman who now lives in California with his new and younger wife. He sends my client a substantial alimony payment each month to atone for his sins. After the usual courtesy greetings and some small talk, the desk phone rings, making me jump.

"Excuse me for calling so late, sir," the desk clerk greets me. I look at the clock, it's only 930pm but maybe that is considered late in Canada, I don't know.

"Not a problem at all. What seems to be the issue?" I ask.

"You have a young lady waiting for you in our bar area, sir. She asked that I ring and ask you to join her. May I tell her to expect you? I asked her name, but she said you were expecting her."

"Oh, yes, of course. I wasn't expecting her until tomorrow. I will be down momentarily. Please see that you send a drink for her or anything else she needs while she waits."

"Very good, sir. I'll see to it, please ring me if you need anything at all," he says, hanging up.

I race around the room, putting on dress shirt and trousers, thankful I have already showered. It must be Grace. How bold of her! I never would have expected her to search me out. I didn't tell her I was staying at the Ritz either and I'm not registered under my real name. Suddenly, I start to worry. Who the hell is waiting for me in the bar? I glance around my room and see an ice pick on the bar. I grab it and place it in my jacket pocket, just in case. As I walk out the door, my laptop is pinging with messages from the divorcee in Arizona. Not now, sweetheart, your money can wait.

The desk clerk greets me as I exit the elevator and guides me to the bar area. The restaurant and bar are very full tonight. I glance around the bar as we enter, and don't see anyone resembling Grace. The clerk motions toward a young woman with cropped brown hair like a man's cut. She is poorly dressed and looks very out of place at the Ritz. In fact, I'm surprised they let her in. She has a messenger bag across her body and looks like she is enjoying the bottle of beer I must have bought for her.

"You requested to see me, miss?" I ask, not moving to sit down.

"Oh yeah, they wanted me to be sure you had actually come to Montreal. So, I guess now I can tell them that I've laid eyes on ya." She takes another swig from the bottle.

"Is that all you need?" I am really annoyed.

"Do you have a ride to your meetings this week? The last time, the guy had trouble showing up, I would not advise that ya not show up, ya know what I mean?"

"Yes, I have proper transportation and a reliable driver, so you tell your people, they have nothing to worry about, you hear me?"

"Yeah, yeah, I hear ya. I just have to check on things, ya know? We must be sure that you can be counted on. Thanks for the drink. See ya around." She hops down from the tall chair and slinks out of the bar back to wherever she came.

I sigh, very aggravated that I was disturbed for that. She couldn't just stake out the place and watch when I arrived? Whoever sent her has very poor taste, first for hiring someone like her and his method of surveillance is pathetic. The bartender brings me a whiskey and water, telling me I look like I need a drink. I thank him and sit at a different table than the dirty street urchin used. The whiskey burns beautifully down my throat. As I tilt my head back, I look across at the restaurant. Tables are full of people obviously having business dinners and a few couples enjoying a nice meal. A loud roar of laughter erupts from a larger group seated near the window. I smile, thinking they are really enjoying themselves. Then I see her.

CHAPTER 44

She's sitting back in her chair, part of the group, but holding back, like there is somewhere else she would rather be. The man to her right, turns her direction and says something to only her. She glances up at him and shakes her head no and then turns to speak with the young lady next to her.

I instantly am on the defense. What did he say to my Grace? I stand but then decide against walking over to her group. Relieved that the bartender didn't see me rise, I take my seat again. I'll just watch for now. Maybe I misinterpreted her reaction to whatever he said. I move my chair so I can get a better angle to see her and wave at the bartender for another whiskey. I ask him for some bread and cheese as well. My stomach is reminding me I haven't eaten since my arrival.

For the next 45 minutes, I eat and slowly nurse my drink, watching the group. Finally, they start to break up. People rising and shaking hands goodbye. It must be a group of pharmacists networking after the conference. Grace rises and I nearly jump out of my seat. She gives a brief hug to the girl next to her and speaks to others near her end of the table. The man who spoke to her earlier had been strangely quiet since the comment I witnessed. Now he is rising too and is helping Grace with her coat. She thanks him, again he leans in and says something. She appears to shake her head and decline his offer. She is now walking away from the table and he quickly says goodbye to the others and moves to follow her. I do the same.

Grace is only a few steps ahead of him and she gets through the revolving door before he can slip in behind her. I see a service entrance to the side and take it so I can get to the street before her. I make it out of the building and walk quickly up to the corner of the block. I don't have my overcoat and the night is brutally cold, but nothing will stop me from making certain this guy doesn't touch her.

My suspicions were right, and he is quickly behind her, speaking again. I hear her tell him no, she is sorry, but wants to remain professional. He isn't taking no for an answer and grabs her elbow. That's all I can take.

"Hey, you there! I believe the lady said she wasn't interested. You didn't understand her?" I step in between them, catching the scent of Grace's perfume, nearly making my knees buckle beneath me.

"Hey man, we were just talking. You need to mind your own business."

"No, I think your conversation is over. Isn't that right, Grace?" I am looking straight into his eyes as I speak and then I turn to look at her.

She smiles and says as cool as the night air, "Oh yes, Immanuel, you are absolutely right. I was beginning to think we wouldn't get to see one another this evening. I'm so glad you were able to keep our plans." She is smiling at me just like I've dreamed for months.

"Shall we, then, my dear?" I ask her, still staring at him, as I offer Grace my arm and we turn to walk toward her hotel. I hear the man swear under his breath, then turn to hail a cab cruising in front of the Ritz.

We don't speak until we turn the corner, out of his sight.

"Immanuel..." she looks up into my eyes, "Finally..."

I don't let her finish. I wrap my arms around her and pull her into my embrace, kissing her hair as she lays her head against my chest. I can't believe this moment is finally here. Even though the temperature must now have dipped into the upper 30s, my entire body feels warm. She suddenly pulls away, aware that I am without a coat.

"Let's go back inside where we can talk," Grace says, smiling, leading me back to the Ritz by holding my hand.

"Yes, let's go inside. We have much to talk about," I agree.

CHAPTER 45

We find the small table in the bar where I was seated previously. It's private and quiet in this corner. I help Grace with her coat and am speechless by how beautiful she is in person and tell her so. I could tell her every single day and it wouldn't do justice to how I feel about her.

"Are you prepared for your lecture, Grace?"

"Yes, I am, as much as I possibly can anyway. I'm a little nervous about it, I'm presenting about a new narcotic that is less addictive. There are some pharmacists that have strong feelings about putting more narcotic drugs into the market when there's such an international problem with addiction. I'm honestly not sure how much ownership pharmaceutical developers have regarding addiction. I think that responsibility lies on the prescribing physicians. So, there's always some challenging questions that are raised for speakers on this topic."

"I'm sure you are very well prepared to handle anything they throw at you."

"Well, we will see. When did you arrive, Immanuel?"

"Today. This afternoon, actually. I was in my room and realized I hadn't eaten since leaving Nigeria, so I came down for a drink and a bite and then I saw you with that group."

"I must properly thank you for helping me with that man. He didn't seem to want to accept no for an answer."

"Well, who can blame him? You are an incredible woman, Grace. I'm sure he is smitten, just like me."

Grace blushes and moves a strand of hair behind her ear. "I truly do appreciate you coming to my rescue, Immanuel."

"You have rescued me Grace. I will always be in your debt." I smile and try to take her hand, but she changes the subject.

"Are you staying here at the Ritz?"

"Yes, I'm here on business so thankfully I'm not the one to foot the bill at this place," I say, smiling, "It's lovely, isn't it?"

"Yes, it's perfect. I've never stayed at a Ritz Carlton' it's a treat just to be in the lobby and restaurant. The food was exquisite."

"Would you like anything to eat now, Grace? Or another drink?"

"No, thank you Immanuel. I really should get back to the Omni. I need to be in the speakers' lounge at 730 in the morning. After I speak, I'm free though. If you are available, I'd love to see you."

"Of course. I have cleared my schedule for only us tomorrow. I'll walk you to your hotel, but before we go, I want to ask you for a dance."

Grace glances at the musicians playing and the few couples in the dance area. "I would like nothing more, Immanuel."

I motion to the concierge and ask for my overcoat to be brought down and then I escort my love to our first dance. Hesitating, I try to remember everything I have seen in movies and on YouTube, hoping she will forgive me for any missteps. There is no need for forgiveness though, she fits perfectly into my embrace and we move like we have been dancing together our entire lives. She notices too and smiles up at me, drawing me closer. I am oblivious to anyone else on earth with her in my arms.

The song ends too soon but she must get some rest before her presentation. I am handed my overcoat and we are quickly outside, huddling together against the cold.

"I really could get a car, Immanuel. It's so cold tonight, and I know you aren't used to this temperature," she says teasing me.

Our walk is all too brief. We slip inside the lobby of the Omni and I walk with her to the elevators to say goodnight. She turns to me and I take a chance. I slip my hand around her and bend to kiss her. She offers no resistance and any tension between us is instantly gone. I keep it brief though and ease away.

"I'll be in touch with you tomorrow Grace. Sleep well. I know you will give an incredible presentation," I say, slowing walking backward and letting our hands slowly slip apart.

"Sleep well, Immanuel. Thank you again for tonight," she says and then steps into the elevator.

I am joyous walking back to my hotel. My feet don't feel like they are touching the ground. I sing to myself, then whistle, then do an American football touchdown dance.

"I LOVE HER!!!" I yell at the top of my lungs into the night. Cars honk, people stare, and some homeless guy laughs and says, "Don't we all, buddy! Don't we all?!" offering me a high five. Instead of a high five, I hand him a hundred-dollar bill.

"Damn, you weren't kidding. You really do love her!" I hear him say as I move further down the street.

CHAPTER 46

The next morning at 8:55 am, I slip into the conference room with the stolen name tag clipped to the pocket of my jacket. I dressed as I think a pharmacist would and from the looks of the crowd, I nailed it. White dress shirt, tie, black jacket, and slacks; I look scholarly and fit in just fine. I feel butterflies in my stomach at the anticipation of seeing Grace again. Just a few minutes more, I tell myself. I see the expert panel on the stage and a gentleman who appears to be the emcee to keep it all on schedule. He approaches the lectern and introduces the next speaker: my Grace. He basically reads her bio printed in the program, but that's okay, he could never do her justice anyway.

Then she walks out on the stage. I can't breathe as I sit forward in my seat. She is dressed in a light pink fitted dress with a black belt and heels. Her hair is swept up in the back with just a few strands framing her face. She looks amazing. I didn't even hear her opening remarks; I'm so spellbound. I have to refocus so I can remember every word.

She addresses the conference like a true professional. I notice the attention of the audience members, an occasional head nod, and note taking. They are intrigued by the new narcotic drug her company developed. She presents the comprehensive data demonstrating lower dependency and better pain management. She then moves to the financial data and then the attendees on the business side of pharmacy are taking notes.

I am sitting back in my seat with a huge smile across my face. I am so proud of her. I knew she was incredible at her job but seeing her at work like this is more than I imagined. She wraps up with about five minutes to spare and offers to answer a few questions. A few conference attendees in the crowd raise their hands waiting for her to point to them. I raise mine as well.

She looks across the crowd and our eyes meet. I see her look down and blush.

"You sir, in the back left of the room. Your question please," Grace nods in my direction.

"Philip Vellore speaking, thank you for this information. I enjoyed your session very much. Does your company plan for this drug to be placed in market worldwide, with the appropriate approvals, of course?"

"Thank you, Mr. Vellore. Yes, of course, we are excited to share our development with patient and health care providers in the world market. This conference was one of the first steps of our plan to do so,"

"Then I'd like to speak with more after the conference, please. I'll let you answer some other questions now. Thank you again, this information is very good." With that, I walk away from my seat toward the back of the room to wait for Grace. I hear her indicate to the room she can take one more question and someone in the front steps forward to speak. I am no longer listening, only watching. Within a few minutes she ends and thanks everyone for their time.

There is another speaker immediately following Grace, so she can step away from the stage without anyone approaching her. As she walks to the back of the room, her eyes are fastened on me, and sparkling.

"You were fantastic. Can you leave?" I offer her my arm and start to move toward the door.

"Thank you, Immanuel or should I say Phillip Vellore? I must say I was surprised to see you. I didn't know you had such an interest in pharmacy. Yes, let's step out," she accepts my arm.

"I have an interest in you. The rest is just extracurricular. Are you hungry? And I thought we could go to the museum of art down the street."

"That sounds lovely. I've never been but have admired the building since I arrived. Let me get my coat from my room, would you like to walk up with me?"

"Of course, I don't want you to be out of my sight for a moment."

CHAPTER 47

Her room is well organized. All her clothes are hanging in the closet, her laptop and briefcase placed neatly on desk. She offers to fix me a drink and even though it's ten in the morning, I accept. She then excuses herself to freshen up before we go.

I reach into my jacket pocket to pull out the envelop for Grace. Inside, is fifteen thousand American dollars. I am going to tell her the truth about what happened.

I am standing by the window watching people on the street and finishing my drink when she emerges looking even better than before. The stress of the presentation is behind her and she looks fresh and relaxed. She walks up to me and takes my drink from my hand, placing it on a nearby table. Without speaking, she wraps her arms around my waist. I embrace her and pull her close to me. We stand, looking into one another's eyes for a moment before she tilts her face up to mine. Leaning forward, I kiss her soft lips. I feel myself melting into her, completely at her mercy.

All too soon, she pulls away, breathless. I keep her within my arms, and I decide now is the time to tell her about the money.

"Grace, I need to talk to you about something that happened," I start.

"Yes, of course, Immanuel. What is it?"

"You remember that I asked you about your finances and if you were okay?"

"Yes, why?"

"I know what happened to your money," I look into her eyes and watch them fade from bright blue to a darker, frightening color.

She turns away from me and walks to the reading chair near her bed. She sits, wrapping her arms around her body, looking very small and cold.

"Grace, look at me, please, it wasn't me, I swear to you" I stammer, trying to think of the right way to approach this.

"I don't want to look at you, Immanuel. Please, don't tell me you were involved, I convinced myself it was a random thing after we started talking again. I have just started trusting you in these past few months. Just say what you need to say. I've been through so much this year, you know that. I don't know if I can handle anything else," she pauses, "You know all I ever wanted from you was the truth. After everything you have put me through, you owe me that, Immanuel."

"I owe you more than the truth, Grace. I owe you everything. And I will be sure that you always have my everything, whatever you need. Here's the truth, this is exactly what happened...."

She sits in the chair with her legs tucked up under her and listens without looking at me as I tell her everything. I tell her how romance scammers work, their common methods, what they do when their appeals to good will giving doesn't work. I tell her about the links, keylogging, man in the middle, SIM swaps, all of it. I confess that I sent her the links when we first started talking; before we learned more about one another. I insist to her I fell in love and never intended to take anything from her. I was an idiot and didn't remove the connections to her that I placed when Amobi "borrowed" my laptop. I told what I did to him when he told me what he had taken.

"I have ransacked his entire apartment and taken all hardware, anything that could have your information on it, Grace. I assure you, there's nothing to worry about now. But when you return home, I want you to change your accounts, all of them, just to be sure. I beg your forgiveness, Grace. I never wanted to harm you in any way. After your first email, I knew you were different, and I would never scam you. I only wanted you. I have something for you, Grace, please take this, even if you never want to see me again," I lean back in the office chair, exhausted from my confession and hand her the envelope.

"I suspected it was you when my bank called me, Immanuel. Neither the bank nor I could prove anything though. I told you they restored nearly all of my funds." At least she is speaking to me. She holds the envelop in her hands.

"Aren't you going to open it, Grace?"

"Yes, ok… I am," she says. Her hands are shaking as she tears the side of the envelop open and counts the money that had exchanged into US dollars. "Immanuel, you don't have to do this, I told you my funds were returned.

"That was the bank's money. This is yours. I retrieved this from the man who took it from you and am returning it to you. I won't take it back. I know this is my fault. Take this as assurance that I will protect you and never hurt you again." I tell her, relieved to see that she is finally looking at me. I have another fifty thousand in my room to give her, but since she doesn't know that she is missing that money, I will figure out how to return that to her later.

"Immanuel, you have no idea what I have been through. Do you know what it's like to feel like you have been attacked by a someone you can't see? I was taken advantage of, and when I tried to fight back or at least scream out, there's no one there. Do you know how it feels to love someone and then open your eyes and that person never existed? All the memories I have are a vapor. All the words, songs, poems; it's like I'm standing in the bitter Nebraska winter and I saw the words come out of someone's mouth and they disappear into the air. It's like a dream. We made a life together, Immanuel. It was so real to me, but I awoke, and the bed was empty. It would have been easier to know you died, at least I would have had closure. But no, I thought I had lost my mind. I was in love with an imaginary man. Do you know what that feels like? Tell me, Immanuel. Have you ever thought about the person on the other end, hanging on your every word? I laid awake at night, praying you were safe. I thought about your son, your home, your favorite foods, everything about you. I imagined what it would be like to meet you at the airport in DC when your duty ended. Did you ever stop to think about how your story would end? I guess you would have just disappeared, never giving me another thought," Grace pauses, her anger finally apparent.

"No, I could never allow myself to think…."

"Of course not. You couldn't stop to think. You wouldn't want to hurt or feel guilty. After all, your victims have money, so they don't have feelings, right? Is that it?"

"Grace, I'm so sorry, I have no excuse. I'm so very sorry to you and everyone I've ever hurt. You are right. In Nigeria, as I told you, there are no jobs for most of the population and I saw this as the only way to survive. If I was fortunate enough to find a job, it wouldn't pay a decent wage. This is a way that we can provide for ourselves and for our families. I know it's wrong. Believe me, I know it's wrong, Grace."

"I had to find you, Immanuel. I would have spent the rest of my life trying to find you and to know your truth. Do you know what it is like to sort out what is real and what isn't about someone you love? I was a fool at first, but you weren't going make me a fool for the rest of my life. I had to know you, the real you. Honestly, I think that you are somewhat relieved that I found you. I don't think you have ever felt safe to be yourself."

"I was very frightened when you messaged me after you discovered what I was. I thought you would come after me, maybe even turn me in. Grace, when we talked, I didn't feel like a scammer. I felt special. I wanted you to speak to me, Immanuel, not Andrew. You made me want an honest life. I wanted to be someone you might love someday. I want to protect you, always. As long as I have breath in my body, I swear to you, I will protect you."

"So where does this leave us, Immanuel? You must not think I'm going to turn you in, or you wouldn't be here now."

"Just like you said, you want to understand more than you want revenge, Grace. And I believe that is truly what you want. Revenge isn't in your heart. If it was, you would have destroyed your husband when you learned of his infidelity. And you would have already destroyed me. You are smart and can take care of yourself. I have no doubt of that. But your heart is too good. I told you, your love has made me a changed man."

"What do you mean, a changed man?"

"I've changed. I'm not going to live that life anymore," I swallow, feeling guilty for my lie. I had spent most of the previous evening chatting with clients. Can I really walk away? It's the only way to support myself I have ever known. "I have some meetings tomorrow and the day after and when I return to Nigeria, I am starting a new life. I don't know exactly what I'll do yet, but I'll figure it out."

"I am hopeful for you Immanuel. I really am. I know you can become whatever you set your mind to be. I hope you will let me know what you decide."

"We will speak every day. I'll have no secrets from you, ever," I say and slowly move to take her hand in mine. I thank the almighty God when she doesn't pull away.

"Let's keep our plans today, Immanuel. I'd like to see the museum while we are here." She stands and pulls me up next to her.

"Grace, I will forever be in your debt. Anything you want is yours," I smile, looking into her blue eyes.

"Then you will take me dancing tonight. You owe me more than just one dance. That will be the first step in your penance," she laughs, "We should go now, we have at least half the day left," she smiles.

"And some of the night, I hope. Let's get something to eat on our way, I'm famished."

CHAPTER 49

We find a small café on the street between the Omni and the museum. I ask Grace to order for me and I excuse myself to make a call to Pierre. He answers at the first ring. This guy wasn't kidding, he really is at the ready for anything I need.

"Immanuel! How are you, my friend? Is there anything wrong with your room? Are you eating well? What can I do for you?"

"Pierre, I am very well. I need you to get a blue evening dress from my room and take it to the Omni for my friend to wear this evening. Please have their concierge place it in her room. I also need you to drive us this evening," I instruct him, giving him Grace's room number.

"I'll go right away, sir. Anything else?"

"No, I'll text you with the time I want to be picked up. That is all for now, thank you for your help, Pierre," I say as we sign off. I appreciate working with people like Pierre. He doesn't ask questions; only does what is asked of him and does it immediately.

I return to the small table where Grace and I will share our first meal. The waiter is there, appreciating that Grace is ordering in French. I sit back and watch her, thinking how blessed I am to be here.

"Is everything okay, Immanuel?" she asks, after the waiter has walked away.

"Yes, I was just asking the concierge to provide some suggestions for our dinner and dancing tonight. Is there somewhere you would like to eat?"

"Yes, there is. The Renoir restaurant at the Ritz. I want a table overlooking the terrace. Their food is said to be exquisite, like you are actually in France.

"Then that's what we will do. I like a woman who knows what she wants."

"I like a man who lets me decide what I want," she says, smiling.

The atmosphere at the small café is peaceful. It's midweek, so there are only a few other couples dining and we are granted plenty of privacy. We eat our food slowly, enjoying each other's company. We order a tiramisu to share for dessert as a cool breeze picks up and the sun moves behind a cloud. Grace tries to hide a shiver.

I move my chair around the small table so I'm sitting by her side rather than across from her. I slip my arm around her, shielding her from the cooler air.

"Thank you, Immanuel. It just got really cool without the sunshine."

"Why don't we cancel dessert and go on to the museum? The little walk will warm us up," I say, motioning to the waiter.

I explain to him that I'd like the check. His face suddenly shows concern that something wasn't to our liking, but we assure him everything was perfect. It's just time for us to go. I provide him with payment for the meal while Grace gathers her purse and secures her coat around her. We are soon walking hand in hand down the sidewalk toward the museum.

Grace and I pass on the museum's guided tour, preferring to wander together on our own. I watch her face as she reacts to various pieces. She spends extra time in the post-impressionism collection. Most of the pieces are of Parisian scenes. She especially likes Monet, Degas and Gauguin. We both like Toulouse-Lautrec and laugh about how scandalous and provocative his subject matter must have been to the public audience at that time.

"I wish we could all be so honest with our expression," Grace comments.

"You sound like you have a regret, my dear, tell me what's on your mind," I prod.

"Oh, well, I don't know. I enjoyed painting in college, but I haven't done so in years. I wouldn't know where to start now. I am not very confident. I always worry that someone wouldn't like my work."

"I would love to see your work. In art, you can't please everyone Grace. I think if you love it, then there will be others who do too. I like to work in my garden. People who have seen it don't necessarily love the plants, flowers, and colors I choose. But I do it because it brings me peace. It's not for them."

"You are right. Of course, I should paint again, even if no one else cares for what I create, it can just be for me."

"And for me. I'd love to experience your art," I tell her as I brush her hair back behind her ear.

She looks up into my eyes and that's all it takes. We are in each other's arms, immediately realizing our time at the museum needs to come to an end. I call for Pierre and within moments he is opening the door of the car in front of the museum, a huge smile on his face, nodding at me in appreciation of this unexpected development.

At the Omni, we barely get inside Grace's room, both of us breathless and saying we can't believe we are finally together. I try to hold back my desire for her, gentle kisses, soft touches, taking our time. She reassures me when I hesitate, letting me advance our love. She is more beautiful than I even imagined when I laid on my bed visualizing her after every chat during the night alone in Nigeria. We confess our love and our intense desire that has been there from the very beginning. At the height of passion, I tell her I want a child with her. She laughs but doesn't stop me, only kisses me deeply.

We spent all afternoon into the evening making love, talking, laughing, and holding one another. We shower together, again finding our passion overtake us. I will never grow tired of this woman. I want her to be by my side until death finds me.

"What is this?" Grace asks as she is getting clothes from her closet.

I'm sitting on the bed, buttoning my shirt and see that she has found the blue gown.

"Ahhh, yes, that is a gift I brought from Lagos. The blue won't do justice, but it reminded me of your eyes. Do you like it?"

"Like it? I love it. Immanuel, it's a Halston. It must have cost you a fortune," she says, never taking her eyes off the dress, evaluating the cut, and running her fingers across the fine fabric.

I stand and walk to her, eager to take her into my arms again. She is too enamored with the dress though to notice me. I smile, pleased to have made her happy.

"I'd like you to wear it tonight, Grace."

"Yes, of course, I wouldn't dream of wearing anything else."

"I'm going to go back to my room so you can get ready. I'll send a car for you in an hour or so, okay?"

"Yes, that will be perfect," she turns to me, "Immanuel, I had the most wonderful day with you. Thank you for today, I'll never forget this."

"Neither will I, Grace. I'll see you soon," holding her hand as I walk to the door and looking back as I depart.

CHAPTER 50

Back in my room, I take a quick shower. My laptop is still powered on from last night. In my rush to get to Grace's conference this morning, I didn't even log off. Another rookie move. I think Enofi is right, I'm getting soft. At the very least, I'm getting careless. I better tighten up my game. I see I have some client emails to answer, but those will have to wait. I pick up the cell phone I use for clients and open the first of an assortment of messaging apps.

The next 30 minutes I spend chatting with a widow in New Mexico. While I wait for her reply, I grow tired of watching the little typing bubbles. I pick up a pen and start sketching on the hotel notepad. I draw some stupid looking people and animals, then a 3d box and other doodles. I rip the paper off and throw it in the trashcan. Good lord, woman, stop typing. I am growing restless. I CAN'T DO THIS ANYMORE! I write this over and over on the notepad, pressing firmly into the pad of paper. Seriously, some clients make me crazy! I glance at the time and message Pierre to bring the car. I'll go with him to retrieve Grace for our evening of dining and dancing.

Ping. Ugh, the widow. I tell her I'm running out of data and must sign off, sending my love and affection. We have been talking for a few months, I think she is almost ready. Her man is going to have a dire need for her generosity in the next week. I'll soon know how much she cares.

Pierre pulls the car up to the valet area of the Omni. I don't wait for him to open my door; I am halfway inside the lobby by the time he gets around the car. I look back see him waiting for me to return with that big I-know-a-secret smile on his face.

I start to walk to the elevator but see a glimpse of blue out of the corner of my eye. Grace is sitting at the bar drinking a glass of red wine.

This is strange. I told her I would escort her from her room. Taking a glance at my Omega watch, I see that I'm ten minutes earlier than the time I told her, just as I had planned. I approach her slowly, so she is sure to see me. When she looks up, her eyes are dark, but she offers me a small smile.

"Honey, what's wrong? Why are you sitting here? Did I not offer to escort you from your room?"

"Yes, you did Immanuel. I'm fine, just needed a drink. While I was in the shower, my husband left me a voice mail. He sounded angry, something about money. I tried to call him back, but he didn't answer."

"He didn't give you more information? Are the children okay?"

"Yes, they are fine. I called Seth and he said the girls are still at soccer practice, but everyone is fine. I also called my secretary and she said he had called the office looking for me too. He hung up, swearing in her ear when she reminded him, I was gone to this conference. Nice of him to remember where I am, right?"

I feel my stomach start to wind into knots. He knows the money Enofi pulled is gone. I need to tell Grace before he calls her back.

"Grace, excuse me, I'm going to make a call. I'll let you finish your drink."

I step away from the bar to a private area but where I can still see her. Damn, it's 4 am in Lagos, there won't be anyone I can contact at the bank. I log on to their customer website to the account Enofi and I share to see if anymore deposits have been made. Shit, there's more money there than when I left and that doesn't include the money I withdrew to return to Grace. This isn't going to stop. She has to close her accounts.

I nearly run back to the bar. "Grace, you have to freeze your accounts right away, all of them, even the ones you have with your husband. You need to contact your cell phone company too. Do you have enough cash and credit cards to get you home?"

"What is going on, Immanuel? Are you involved this time again?"

"Not directly involved, Grace. I know what is happening, but I can't stop it. I can't protect you. Believe me, I want this to stop, I've tried. I've got another fifty thousand in my room that someone took from you. I was going to give it to you tonight. But I can't chase this, it will keep happening until you close your accounts and get rid of your phone, computer, whatever you were on when you clicked those links."

"How could you? The first time wasn't enough? I can't believe I've been so stupid, Immanuel. You did this to me, you started all of this with your lies. It's never going to stop. You have fucking ruined my life!" Grace is shouting in the bar and the staff is looking at us.

"Grace, please, we can't do anything here. Come with me please, let's just go where we can figure this out," I speak quietly to her, so as not to provoke her further. I just want to get her away from here, somewhere quiet, and private. I try to take her arm and she pulls away, but not before I can feel how she is shaking with anger. After a moment, she does stand though and walks with me.

I try to help her slip on her wrap as she is walking, again she pulls away from me, but is struggling to get her wrap situated around her evening gown. I had such a lovely evening planned and it's all gone to hell. The castle I built in the sky is fading, there's no way she will ever trust me.

"Grace, let me help with your wrap…"

"No! Don't touch me. Don't you think you've done enough? Really, Immanuel. I have no idea how you sleep at night. And the disgusting thing is I know that I'm not the only one who has had this happen. At least I can look at the man who ruined my life. The rest of your women are out there worried sick if their knight in shining armor is okay while you are robbing them blind!"

"I didn't do this to you, Grace. I swear. Your information was stolen from my computer or phone or something. It wasn't me, I want to help you, please let me help you, I beg you. Let's go where we can think and talk. You need to try to reach your husband again. You can scream at me, hit me, I deserve it. I'm going to do whatever I can to help you."

Pierre's smile is gone as he opens the door for Grace. Thankfully she gets into the car. Pierre touches my arm, and looks up at me, curious if he is still to take us to the Ritz.

"Yes, Pierre, it's fine. Please just drive us as we had planned," I say softly so Grace can't overhear and decide to go back to her room. She is so angry right now, but I know I can't leave her alone.

Pierre circles a few blocks when he notices that Grace is trying to compose herself. She won't speak to me, but when I offer my handkerchief she accepts, spending a few minutes daubing her eyes and fixing her hair. I want to tell her she looks beautiful but am afraid it will only set her off again.

We arrive at the Ritz and she seems a bit calmer. Pierre opens the door for us, and I ask him to stay close, I'll text him if we need anything. He nods in agreement as he offers Grace his hand as she emerges from the car. She stands and composes herself for just a second. I offer my arm and she allows me to escort her into the building. She walks quickly toward the elevator, pulling me along.

"Would you like anything to eat? I can get it sent up if you like," I ask, my stomach begging for her to say yes, as she pushes the button for the elevator.

"No, I don't feel like eating, Immanuel. I'm surprised you would even ask."

"I don't feel like it either," telling her yet another lie, "I just thought you should eat since you had a glass of wine. It's 10 pm; you last ate at noon."

"I don't need you to tell me when to eat."

At my floor, I take the lead to my room. I barely get the door unlocked and Grace pushes through the door.

"Could I use your restroom please? I need a moment."

"Yes, of course. It's right through here. Take your time," I say, as she shuts the door in my face.

God, I'm an idiot. What the hell am I going to do? I am with her in person after all these months and this had to happen? I pour a drink to try to calm my nerves. I'm starving but I don't dare mention to her that I want to eat. Whisky will have to do for now. In the office area, my laptop is open, and my other cell is flashing with waiting messages. Before I have a chance to move them out of sight, Grace is behind me.

"Would you mind if I sat here at your desk and try to call my husband? I need a little privacy," she asks.

"Of course, I'll take my drink out on the balcony. Take all the time you need."

She smiles a thank you but doesn't speak, only waits for me to leave. There is nothing I can say to reassure her, hell, nothing I can do to reassure myself. I swear I am going to kill Enofi when I get back to Nigeria. He's just doing what we were trained to do; what I have done myself many times over, but it would make me feel better to choke the life out of him.

CHAPTER 51

Sitting on the balcony, I hear Grace speaking to her husband. I'm relieved that she was able to get him on the phone, at least they can discuss what to do. Suddenly, her voice changes, firmer, abrupt, no nonsense. Then I hear him raising his voice, yelling at her. This is no longer about the money. This is about everything. Grace is crying, shouting at him between sobs. I want to rush in there, but I remain seated, trying not to interfere. I've finished my drink but am pretending to sip and not look like I'm listening. This issue isn't my fault nor is it my battle to fight. Silence. Then I hear her talking again to someone else. Her voice is calmer, but she is clearly giving instructions to someone in a cold, calculated way. Silence again. Then another call. Again, she is giving implicit instructions. Whoever she called this time isn't given time to ask questions or argue.

I wonder what to do now… Is she finished with her phone calls? I think I'll wait here, assuming she will come to me when she is ready. I still see her out of the corner of my eye sitting at my desk. She has made herself comfortable in the office chair. If I didn't know what just happened to her, I would think she was just sitting there working. It looks like she is texting or doing something on her phone, but my laptop is open. God, I hope she doesn't touch it, I can see that the screensaver is the only thing hiding more of my secrets.

I hear her once again on the phone. It sounds like she is giving account information. She must be on the phone with her bank fraud line freezing her accounts. At least that will stop the bleeding. It's so cold out here on the balcony. I stand up to get my blood circulating and try to warm up. There are very few cars or people on the street tonight, I guess they didn't want to brave this cold. Turning around and looking back into the room, I notice Grace is no longer at the desk. I decide to brave coming in rather than freezing to death. Once inside, I see the bathroom door is shut. I'll give her some more time, deciding to order room service so my stomach will stop growling.

The food has arrived. I ordered from the French restaurant downstairs where Grace wanted us to dine tonight. I can give her that at the very least. I knock softly on the bathroom door and tell her I have food and wine if she would like some. What feels like an eternity passes and then I hear the door unlock. Grace looks completely composed and fresh.

"Did you bathe? I was getting worried, sweetheart. You look radiant," I can't help it, I have to tell her. How can she look beautiful after all she experienced tonight? I am sure I look like death.

"No, darling, I didn't. I've been on the phone with my sister and her boss. We were making arrangements to file against my husband for alimony and divorce. When he called, it wasn't really about the missing money. He wanted to talk about that of course but he really wanted to ask me for a divorce because he wants to marry his secretary."

"Oh honey, I'm so sorry," I start, but she stops me.

"Don't be, my love. You know you said earlier that I don't have revenge in my heart, that I am the type to prefer to understand than get revenge? Immanuel, I have known this man since we were in college, I understand him better than he knows himself. As my sister's boss, who is now my lawyer said, I raised his children, entertained his clients, and built his business as much as he did. Now it is time that I'm repaid for being a faithful wife all these years. If you want to call that revenge, fine. But my silence and submission through all that's happened this past year wasn't weakness. In fact, I have perfect understanding about the last year now. I think it will soon be time to close a few chapters of my life. And I know I'm strong enough to take care of myself and not have any regrets."

"I have no doubt about that, none at all. Would you like to eat?"

"No, Immanuel, I don't. And you aren't either. You said you would dance with me. I know it's late, but it's now or never. Let's go downstairs."

"Oh yes, I did promise. Let's go," I grab a small baguette as she takes my hand, and we head downstairs. I'll try to sneak a bite or two when she isn't looking.

The orchestra is playing romantic music, nothing lively this late at night. They are working to create a mood in the air and doing an amazing job. I order a bottle of red wine and we sit sipping and watching the other guests on the dance floor before joining them.

On the dance floor, I take Grace in my arms, cautious of her openness with me. It's like the missing money never happened. Maybe she forgave me, maybe she just wants one more happy night, maybe she just doesn't want to think about that or her soon to be ex-husband. Whatever it is, she is flirtatious, charming, and a joy. The blue dress fits her perfectly, her eyes sparkle reflecting the lights in the ballroom, and her cheeks are blushing from the wine. She is either the strongest person I've ever met or should win an Oscar for best actress. Whatever it is, I love her. I am going to enjoy every second of the rest of my life with this wonderful woman.

We dance until the orchestra stops at almost 2 am. Thankfully my meeting isn't until the afternoon because I don't want this night with her to end.

"Immanuel, do you want to go upstairs? I thought we might continue this."

God, I love her.

"I want nothing more, I only want you, always," I say, even though I'm starting to feel a headache coming on from too much wine and too little food.

We are alone in the elevator and she can't keep our hands off me. We can hardly get to my room fast enough. Once inside, Grace excuses herself and I hear the bath running. This woman....

CHAPTER 52

"Immanuel…. baby…. I need you…" Grace softly calls for me.

I catch my breath as I open the door. She is submerged in the large tub with bubbles up to her neck. Her hair is piled up on top of her head with just a few strands framing her face. She smiles at me and lifts a wet soapy leg up out of the water.

"Won't you join me baby?" she practically purrs to me.

I undress within seconds and join her. She leans back against my chest as I wrap my arms around her, feeling her hands caressing my legs. I lay my head back and close my eyes just enjoying this moment. After a few minutes, Grace has turned around, kissing me, wanting more. I yield to her every move and she knows just how to take me out of this world.

Afterward, we are still lying in the tub when my head begins throbbing. I've been fighting this headache all night. Now the lack of food and sleep and too much wine has won. I moan, shifting in the tub.

"What is it Immanuel? What's wrong?"

"My head feels like it's about to explode."

"Oh, here let me get you something," she offers and I'm too blinded by this pain to argue.

Within minutes she returns with some pills and a glass of water. She is wrapped in the hotel robe sitting on the side of the tub. I feel her place the pills in my mouth and bring the cup to my lips.

"Slowly, slowly, there you go, good. Now just lay back," she places a warm, damp washcloth on my head as I close my eyes. "Just rest there for a bit, that's good. I'll help you get to bed soon, just rest now."

I can sense her moving around in the bathroom and then she goes into the other rooms. I'm so tired. I don't think I've ever felt this tired in my entire life.

Opening my eyes, I realize I must have fallen asleep. The water feels cold now, but I am so drained I can't summon enough energy to move my body. I feel like the room is spinning, almost like I'm looking through a tunnel. I hear Grace return and begin to speak to me.

"Andrew…Can I call you that for old times' sake, Immanuel? Yes? Ok, Andrew? You have messages waiting for you. You can check them once you have rested. Don't worry, I didn't read them, I just heard all the notifications. You are a busy man aren't you, Andrew? Do you think you'll ever stop scamming and do something else? No? You say there's no other opportunities to make money in Nigeria? Yes, I remember…. you told me how it is in your country…. you're right, I understand, there's no other way. Sometimes that's what life gives us, right Andrew? No other way? You said I crave understanding and not revenge. I assure you; I know there's no other way for me either. The problem is, though, I don't think those people waiting for your reply would understand the way I do. Would you tell them your truth? And what happens to them after you move on? Someone needs to protect them, don't you agree?"

"What is it, my darling? Your cloth is cool now? Here I'll warm it up. There now…is that better? Yes, I thought so. Just lay back and let me help you. You once asked me to save you. Do you remember, Andrew? It was after I learned your truth, you asked me to save you. We can only save ourselves, Andrew. It seems you aren't willing to do that though. And I doubt that all those people who have messages waiting for you tonight can save you either. Let me help you. I loved you, the real you, Immanuel. I think I'm the only one you ever allowed to love the real you. I always will love you, but my love isn't enough to make you change. I think Andrew needs to go away; he isn't good for you. Lay back, my love and rest. Let me help you. Let me save you."

Everything is so foggy. Is the bathroom full of steam? It can't be, I feel too cold. The cloth slips just a bit and I see Grace crying. Why is she crying? What is she saying? I'm so tired. I feel myself slipping down into the water, my head is going under. She is sitting right there; can she hear me? She has her hand on the cloth on my head. It's pressing so hard on my throbbing head. Pushing, pushing me down. The cloth feels like it weighs a ton. I can't make my arms work to pull myself up though. Grace, Grace! Why can't I make any words come out of my mouth? I close my eyes as I feel my head slipping all the way under the soapy water.

CHAPTER 53

Mid-States Psychiatric Hospital

Phillips, Dean, MD, PhD   Progress Notes.   Created: 10/20/21 1415

Specialty: Clinical Psychologist Signed: {electronic}   10/20/21 1700

See patient chart for signed Consent to Treat, Privacy Practices and agreement to Hospital Financial policy.

Psychology Clinical Note
Patient: Grace Elizabeth Mullen
DOB: 01/31/1978
DOS: 10/20/21
Inpatient Psychiatric Ward, Room 305
Mid-States Psychiatric Hospital
Self-Admit

Summary: Grace Elizabeth Mullen is a 43 y.o. female. Patient is alert and oriented x3. Her speech is fluid. Patient is cooperative and with appropriate eye contact with occasional looking away into the room when recalling recent events. Patient denies suicidal ideations or thoughts of self-harm.

Disclosure: She is a long-time family friend. She requested self-admission after numerous psychosocial and familial stressors over approximately the last one year.

Patient holds PharmD degree and has full time employment. She has been employed by the same company for the last fifteen years. She also teaches in an adjunct professor position at a local university.

Patient is married, although separated and has consulted with a divorce attorney referred to her by her sister. She plans to seek legal separation and then divorce due to her husband's reported infidelity.

Patient has three children: Sarah, 17, Tabitha, 16, whom they call Tabby, and Seth 14. All are healthy and reported to be handling their parents' separation in a healthy way. We have held one counseling session with Grace and the children. I recommend family counseling to continue after discharge.

Patient states that she and her husband have had money stolen from their bank accounts. She has fraud and identity theft insurance and the money has been restored but she states that she has become fixated with worry about other people who experience such theft. She states she is financially stable and does not have concerns about her income, investment portfolio or savings. She states that hearing stories of fraud and scamming is now a trigger for her.

Mood is generally calm. She appears well-nourished and denies pain at this inpatient assessment. LMP was approximately 2 months ago and denies use of birth control. Symptoms include fatigue, restlessness, anxiety/worry about the future. Some possible psychoses related to travel to Montreal for a pharmacy conference. She was a featured speaker for her company. She stated her employer was adamant that her presentation about a new opioid be a success. Patient states this was stressful for her and she spent months preparing. She feels that it was well received but it is a new drug in the US market, so the marketability is unknown. She feels under pressure by her employer to help advance it to international markets.

Reflecting on her time in Montreal for the conference, patient states that she can see a man being removed by a coroner from his room. She stood on the sidewalk at the back of the hotel and watched. She relates that she was unable to look away, even when she wanted to. She is not confused by this; people die every day. She states that she is sorry it had to happen to him. I asked her if she knew this person. She said no, she does not know who he really is, he is just someone she thought she knew. She states that seeing his lifeless body gave her peace as she watched them take him away and the snow fell on the ambulance gurney, but she also felt a great loss. She said she knows this man didn't like cold weather and it was ironic how the snow was falling on his lifeless body. She states she keeps replaying that scene in her mind. I asked if she was projecting her experience with her mother's death onto this man's demise. She stated no, her mother's death was natural, and she felt like there was a reason this man's death had to happen.

I ask her about her grief over her mother's death this year. She describes it as a shock but is now able to speak about her without crying. She feels a strong connection to both her father and sister, and they have become closer since her mother's death. She misses her mother very much and states there are so many things she wishes she would have told her. She said her mother always gave her the best advice.

She talks about the future in a positive manner. She talks about visiting her father and sister more often now that she is separated and traveling with her children. She also wishes to travel alone and meet people. In particular, she speaks often of traveling to Africa. She states she has heard many things about Western Africa specifically and would like to see if things she has heard are true.

Patient states that she is not grieving over her separation and possible divorce. She states that she has tried to do the right thing for long enough and she wants to focus on her own needs and not worry so much about others. We discussed establishing a healthy balance of self-care and helping others, she also may benefit from setting more boundaries in her life. She agreed to evaluate the time she devotes to family, work, herself, and new relationships.

{Pause in dictation}

"I am so curious about this vision of a deceased man being removed from his hotel. Why is she so fixated on this event, imagined or not?" I sat wondering and thinking to myself. "I have known Grace for most of her adult life, even attended her wedding. She is a very empathetic person but her statements that his death had to happen are intriguing. Was it someone she met briefly at the conference? Or did this event even happen?"

I recall my old friend, Charlie Markham. I met him when I was in residency in Montreal during my ER rotation. We would see each other at the pub sometimes. We both loved hockey but hated the Canadiens. We had to band together, there was no other way to survive when we watched the match in the pub. He was a city cop then, but now, hmmm, let me think, he has had a few promotions in the last few years. Is he a lieutenant now?

Digging through my clinic bag full of files, work in progress research publications, my laptop, and of course, snacks, I find my old flip cell phone. It still works and I haven't taken the time to upgrade. Besides, it gives my medical students something to laugh about. There it is. Charlie's number is still in my contacts. I decide to give him a call. I'm intrigued to know if there were any deaths such as Grace describes during her conference.

"Charlie! Hey buddy, it's Dean Phillips. Yeah, yeah, I can't believe I still have your number either. You have mine too, huh, since you knew it was me! Yeah, yeah, I know, we need to get together and have a drink. I promise, yeah, I'll get to Montreal soon and we will do that. Hey, I know you are busy; congrats on the promotion, by the way, is it lieutenant? Nice man, that's terrific! I'm proud for you. So, I really need a favor. I need to know if you had any deaths during the first week of October in your downtown hotels, say the Omni?"

He tells me to hold on, he'll look. He remembers one, but he didn't think it was the Omni. I wait while listening to him breathe into the phone and punch keys on a computer.

"Oh, not the Omni, but the Ritz? What was the deal? Can you tell me?"

"No, I don't have any leads for you. I just have a patient that was there for a conference and saw a corpse being wheeled out of a hotel. The patient had some pretty intense life events recently, so she is under my care. But she keeps talking about seeing this happen. I just was curious if it's psychosis or someone really did die during her stay."

"Ok, what did you find? Is he real?"

"Black man, unknown age, early 30s. Numerous passport and IDs, none of which are authentic. No wallet, credit cards, or cash found in the room. No laptop or cell? Good grief, how did he even get a room?"

"The clerk said he checked in alone using one of the IDs, I see. A note? So, you think it was a suicide? He wrote, "I CAN'T DO THIS ANYMORE!" over and over? Yes, that certainly sounds like a suicide note. So, how did he die?"

"Oh, yes, how tragic. Alcohol and opioids never mix, you're right. And in the tub? He drowned? What a shame, yes, a terrible thing. No records found for his fingerprints. Hmmm. And even more unfortunate, he will be buried as a John Doe. He could be from anywhere."

"Yes, it's a shame. Well, my friend, thank you for this information. I think had my patient observed the removal of this man from the hotel without the other traumatic events in her life, she wouldn't have given him a second thought."

"Thanks Charlie, I owe you. I'll buy you a pitcher when I'm in Montreal. Take care now."

{Resume dictation}

Assessment and Plan: Continue hospitalization x 1 week to treat fatigue and continue individual counseling.

Art therapy daily as patient has shown significant interest.

Encourage visits from children, father and sister.

Discourage visits from estranged spouse at this time, but not deny visit if desired by patient.

Recommend individual and family counseling post discharge.

Routine labs ordered daily

Pregnancy test ordered due to skipped menses this month/may be due to stress, but patient has reported AM nausea

Nutrition/dietary consultation-no restrictions advised

Screening for suicidal and/or self-harm ideations x2 daily

Electronically signed:
Phillips, Dean MD, PhD on 10/20/21 1710

Made in the USA
Monee, IL
09 April 2022